I0567534

TOUGH MUTHAS!

A NOVEL

BRIAN ANTONSON

Copyright 2014 The Good Word
All rights reserved. No part of this publication may be
reproduced or transmitted in any form or by any means,
electronic or mechanical, including photocopy, recording or any
information storage and retrieval system now known or to be
invented, without permission in writing from the publisher,
except by a reviewer who wishes to quote brief passages in
connection with a review written for inclusion in a magazine,
newspaper, broadcast or online service.
ISBN-13: 978-1-928-076-01-8
ISBN-10: 1928076017

THIS BOOK IS A WORK OF FICTION.
INCIDENTS, NAMES, CHARACTERS
AND PLACES ARE PRODUCTS OF THE
AUTHOR'S IMAGINATION AND USED
FICTITIOUSLY. RESEMBLANCES TO
ACTUAL INCIDENTS, NAMES,
CHARACTERS AND PLACES
ARE STRICTLY COINCIDENTAL.

PART 1
FRIENDS

EVERYONE HAS BEEN talking about the first-ever all-Canadian Super Bowl, featuring Redmond "Red" Crossley, the running back for the Bayporte Invaders of the National Football League. Of course, many people, while talking about it, dislike the matchup of the Invaders versus the Toronto Stars.

Well, *I* am Red Crossley, and I'm writing these words because I have signed a book agreement to write about my experiences with the Invaders. I want to tell the world, or at least those people who want to hear, about being part of the NFL's expansion into Canada.

I'm writing this book on a MacBook Pro laptop computer whenever I'm not preparing for Super Bowl Sunday against the Stars. I need to point out a few things now, to avoid much confusion later on.

The Bayporte Invaders, of Bayporte, Great Elizabeth, Canada, used to be the Detroit Lions.

The Toronto Stars, until fairly recently, had been the Buffalo Bills. Before the commencement of the season, the NFL had chosen Great Elizabeth Place, the Invaders' stadium, as the site of this year's Super Bowl. Most American sports purists disliked the Stars' and Bills' departures to Canada, just as they resented seeing Major League Baseball expand into the Great White North. Especially when the Toronto Blue Jays won two consecutive World Series.

But here is what happened: the two Canadian teams made it into the Super Bowl, as if the Americans had been shut out of their own game.

Bullshit, I say.

My best friend and teammate, Flash Gortton, is the only Canadian on the team besides me. Most of the other guys are white or black and from the American Midwest or Deep South. A man is simply whoever he chooses to be. We have a joke about why we got into football. Whenever someone asks us about it, we'll say, "We don't like football that much. We just like being tackled by big black guys."

When Flash and I started playing for the Invaders and gradually helped the team become a winner, there were labor disputes and plenty of talk about teams' moving to different markets for financial reasons. Everyone seemed to have an issue: one top quarterback wanted more money, and some hotshot wide receiver wanted ten bucks more than that top quarterback did. Agents stood in the dressing room, doing deals with players who were taping up their ankles. The online news services ran stories about how the NFL's expansion into Canada had harmed the league and, over time, might even destroy it. The Canadians had their own league, such as it was, and needed to be content with that.

Then Flash stood on a bench in our locker room and spoke to all of us. Everyone acknowledged that Flash had Hall of Fame talent, but few, besides me, knew of his big-heartedness.

"I think we have some things we need to talk about right now," he said.

A bunch of us lay sprawled about. One of us, Pol Pott, our offensive guard from Arizona, belched as he clipped his tonenails.

Flash nodded. "Pol's in. Who else?"

L.T. Briggs, our mammoth tackle, let forth a vicious blast of flatulence. Once the laughter subsided, Flash continued.

"We have a winning team here, and some people just don't like it. A team in Canada that's beating the Americans. But we need to ignore that and just play football as best we can."

Pol Pott said, "Does that mean if we have to play hard even if we have a hangover?"

Everyone laughed some more.

Flash smiled. "Afraid so, Pol."

"Only L.T. don't have to play hard. He's just got to show up without takin a shower."

L.T. Briggs, the smelliest player I have ever known, is six feet something and closing in on three hundred pounds. I've heard that when L.T. played college football in New Mexico, he kept a pit bull as a pet in his dorm room and, rather than use the washroom like everyone else, he would dump his stool and feces out his window onto the lawn below. He claimed that he saved the school on fertilizer. Myself, I would never have said to his face that he smelled like anything but a pine forest after a gentle rain, mainly because I depended upon his protection on the football field.

We tell everyone that L.T. stands for Lotsa Trouble because he represents that to our opponents. Actually, his initials stand for Laurence Tiffany, but we don't talk about that.

Flash went on some more about how he had to hang together as a team and forget about being a collection of Canadians and Americans, white and black, whatever we were besides being

Bayporte Invaders. Everyone seemed to agree with him, so he kept his talk brief.

"We have a rainbow coalition here," said Flash. "I don't care about anyone's color or nationality. I'm not into racial guilt. I see us as just a bunch of football players with a common goal, and if anyone doesn't like what country we play in, tough shit for them. We need to get stoned together and laid together. We need to be honest with each other and trust one another. That's how we can win together."

Flash paused, to let his words sink in, and for a few moments looked at Pol Pott.

"Are we going to be a team?" Flash asked.

Pol Pott looked up at him and said, "If I want to get some white poontang, can I count on your help?"

Everybody laughed long and hard.

"All I'm saying is that we need to live as a team if we want to play as a team," Flash said, "and anyone on our team who doesn't want to play and live as a team, can go straight to hell. Or they can play for the Seahawks."

Pol said, "Everyone wants to win, but you make it sound like if a team loses, it's because of the players. There are some bad coaches, too. Understand?"

Flash nodded. "Yeah, and those bad coaches work for the Seahawks." He added that he really didn't have much else to say, except that he believed we needed to speak up whenever we had something on our minds.

Pol Pott said, "I've been thinking that, once I get rich and famous enough to turn white, which movie star I wanna be. I'm thinking right now I'm gonna be a blondy guy like Brad Pitt. He gets all the white pussy."

"I'm going to turn black and be Eddie Murphy," said Flash. "Eddie gets so much white pussy because he makes them laugh."

I am a Caucasian Canadian, a native of Bayporte. I stand just over six feet and weigh about two hundred pounds, and I run pretty fast for a white guy. People told me I looked like the actor Timothy Hutton, before he retired from acting and began directing. My hair is getting a bit grayer every day and I have about five thousand dollars' worth of teeth my dentist has screwed, glued and drilled into my mouth.

My admirers say I have a friendly smile and a folksy sense of humor. My eyes are gray and my complexion is mostly pale. If I wanted to do so badly enough, I could go to a tanning salon and get a bit darker. But I don't want to do so badly enough.

I have shaggy, tameless hair that Sheri Rawson says will probably stay in my head for the rest of my life. I would rather have gray hair than no hair.

I am a stylish player. I keep my helmet polished and don't wear sweatbands or much tape. I'm a white player in a game traditionally dominated by blacks, so I prefer a streamlined, minimal appearance. People have said that if a white guy came along with the speed and agility of Jim Brown, O.J. Simpson and Roger Craig, he could get richer than the Rockefellers by playing football. I suppose I am that player.

My salary is currently higher than I ever thought it would be. Thanks to the Internet, even the most casual sports follower knows how much the Invaders pay me, so I won't mention specific numbers. I'm not bragging, either; my agreement with the publisher was for straight talk, so here it is.

As an All-Canadian running back at Northup University in Bayporte, I had my best friend, Flash Gortton, as a teammate, and of course we play together for the Bayporte Invaders.

My running ability comes from a sincere desire not to be mauled by much bigger men. When our quarterback, Vernon Braithwaite, calls the play and hands me the ball, my instincts take over and I find whichever little hole exists and climb through it.

Enough about me for the moment. My point is simply that I have distinguished myself in the NFL by being a superior white running back.

Flash says that if I had been black, people would have said, "Oh, Red's just another fine black running back. So what?" He's probably right that my blackness would have compromised my marketability. Once in a while I have wanted to be black, if only because so many of my Invaders teammates are blacks who wished they were white. I think people would respect me, or at least fear me, more if I were black. But then, what the hell do I know?

I remember the time that Flash and I learned that blacks were people too. We were showering one afternoon with some black guys in a YMCA in some Midwestern city.

Where Flash and I grew up in Canada, we encountered very few black people, except at athletic events when we went to the States and sometimes not very many even then. When we saw them, all we said was, "How's it goin, eh?" or something.

In Bayporte, the colored people always lived somewhere other than I did. They didn't go into our hangouts.

Anyway, that one afternoon at the inner-city YMCA, as Flash and I showered, some black guys came in and soon we were all lathered up. They said something about using a new kind of soap that, if they scrubbed hard enough, would turn them into blue-eyed blonds, and we all laughed.

I can honestly say that Flash and I have never had anything against blacks nor browns, except for the dipshits who ransacked sections of Los Angeles during the Rodney King riots. When that happened, the TV networks stopped running my favorite sitcoms because they wanted to provide live coverage of the mayhem in southern California. What a pisser!

I have been so busy with beginning this book that I have forgotten to say why, and how, I am writing this book. I think I need to explain these things for my teammates' benefit.

The main reason I'm writing it is that my longtime friend, Snoop Kowalski, insisted that I do it. A veteran Bayporte sports reporter, he mostly edits, or bosses around the editors, of the Bayporte *Sun*'s online sports section.

Snoop believed that I could write a book that would help kids, even, or especially, those who weren't headed for big-time sports careers.

"I can help you with this," Snoop said. "I can be your ghostwriter or collaborator, whatever you need."

Everyone says that children are the hope of the world, even here in Great Elizabeth. If so—and they're not just a bunch of whiny spoiled brats—then I imagine that my book project here may actually be worthwhile. I don't want to sound too self-important about it, but perhaps this book of mine might actually travel through the bookstore or library shelves and enter the mind of some Canadian boys and girls whose parents have taught them to hate Chinks, Pakis and Jews.

Also, I made contact with a New York publisher who signed me up and cut me a substantial check for this book. The only thing that concerns this publisher is that I get this project done soon, while the world still gives a crap about what I have to say.

I trust that the publishing company of Galbraith and Lichtmann will be OK with my mention of their involvement. I turned to Flash Gortton and asked him which publisher liked quality nonfiction. He said that G&L had published many books worth bragging about, so I called them, introduced myself and why I wanted to do business with them.

They put me through right away to the acquisitions editor for celebrity biographies. He practically squealed over the phone and did our deal immediately. The main thing he needed from me, in return for their substantial check, was my promise to deliver the manuscript as soon as I could.

At this moment I'm sitting in an oversized, too-comfortable suite at the Hotel Bayporte, our city's best place to stay, with a glass of Canadian Comfort over ice at my side and my MacBook Pro on my lap. My so-called friends told me that my only hope of writing this book would be to use the puny voice recorder Sheri Rawson offered to lend me, then speak my piece and give her back the voice recorder so that people smarter than myself could transcribe my words and shape them into some sort of book.

I told these so-called friends that I wasn't quite as dumb as I seemed, and just to prove it to them, I took out my MacBook Pro and here I am.

Flash is downstairs at the swimming pool, reading whatever he's downloaded onto his iPad. He does more reading than any five people I've ever met, and he pays attention to which publisher is responsible for which book. So when I asked him about my as-yet-unwritten book, he mentioned G&L immediately. Flash reads whatever he can find, even if it's crap. He says there's no such thing as crap to read, but he lies.

Sheri is poolside, too. The three of us have been together as far back as any of us can remember, but Sheri's relationship with Flash is deeper, or at least different. I guess she loves him half as a friend and half as a lover.

So here I sit, writing my book as Flash and Sheri spend some quality time together downstairs. But don't pity me just because Flash and Sheri have a relationship that in some ways excludes me. At this moment, sitting across from me, is the lovely and talented Ms. Francesca Roff, who has been keeping company with me—us, but mostly me—for the past while.

The delightful Ms. Francesca Roff blushes as I type her name. how does she know I'm thinking of her? No matter; she is sprawled on a sofa with a bottle of wine cooler as she taps on my iPad to see who Tom Cruise has married this week. Francesca Roff, of course, is a breathtaking beauty, almost as fine as Sheri Rawson, who is so stunning that it's easy to think the Creator put her on Earth just to make the rest of us feel ugly.

My only complaint about Francesca is that she comes from Italy and speaks English as a second language. She says "little" as "leetle" and "is" as "ees." That annoys me more than it should.

Francesca comes from Rome or Milan, maybe both. Her father, whom I've met, is quite happy to let the other person pay for dinner even though Father Roff owns half of Rome and probably some of Wall Street. He can bore people shitless with his stories about deals he's done in Europe and complains endlessly about North America's lack of cultural and culinary sophistication.

Sheri tells me that Francesca was educated in Milan's finest stores and majored in Versace and Armani. At least she didn't get a Ph.D. in recreational chemistry.

Well, Francesca's current field of study is Red Crossley, and I have to give her credit for having good taste in men. If she weren't such a selfish, spoiled little cunt with snobbish parents, I might even consider marrying her.

She just flipped me off. How did she know I was writing about her?

NOW I WANT to talk to you about why Flash, Sheri and I are staying here in the Hotel Bayporte when we all reside about a dozen blocks from the hotel. As I've said, the Bayporte Invaders, for the first time, have made it into the Super Bowl with the other Canadian NFL franchise, the stuck-up Toronto Stars. Plus, we're going to play the big game at Great Elizabeth Place here in Bayporte.

They're laughing about this throughout Canada, of course.

NFL Commissioner Gabe Roder has gotten plenty of flak over this matter. People say that his predecessors would have prevented it, as if an "all-Canadian Super Bowl" were an American tragedy. Commissioner Roder seems all right to me. I think he has a thankless job. When Ed Blumke, Roder's predecessor, resigned to become a U.S. Congressman, some people opposed Roder's candidacy for the NFL's top job. But after dozens of rounds of voting, the teams' owners grew tired of the balloting and elected Roder.

Once in, Roder approved the sale of the Detroit Lions so they could become the Bayporte Invaders. He also permitted the Buffalo Bills to become the stuck-up Toronto Stars, two big, controversial changes, long overdue.

"The Canadian markets were ready for NFL franchises," Roder said. "We were just dealing with supply and demand." As far as I'm concerned, Gabe Roder is a decent guy who's always trying to do the right thing. He, Flash and I have chased many women together.

Flash has just come back up for a moment. He says that L.T. Briggs has been acting out down by the pool and it's amusing as all hell. L.T. decided he would be more comfortable skinny-dipping, so he pulled off his XXXL-sized swimsuit and asked some old Jewish woman to hold it for him so nobody would steal it. When a security guard came by and insisted that L.T. put it back on, L.T. told him it was a free country and he would stay naked as long as he felt like it.

Flash added that there were plenty of Bayporte wannabe models and actresses down there for my ogling pleasure.

I told him I wanted to write some more and fantasize about some of the perversions I would perform later on Francesca Roff.

"Have you written yet how we're going to destroy the stuck-up

Stars?" he asked.

"They already know that."

"Put it into your book that I would beat the stuck-up Stars almost singlehandedly," he said. "Also that I would make Painless look like a bloody fool out there and that fifty thousand fans would laugh at him."

"Done," I said. I don't think anyone has ever embarrassed Jethro Payne—known to all as Painless—on the field, and I've watched him for hours on DVD. Flash also says he's going to slam into Pain and knock him unconscious. Yeah, right.

Jethro Painless, a safety for the stuck-up Stars, which means that he hangs back there in the secondary and nails whichever guy comes remotely near him with the ball. He got his nickname at the University of Washington, where he put opponents instantly to sleep with one "painless" hit.

Painless is among the best players in the NFL, one of the very few defensive players to win the Heisman Trophy, the fancy, coveted award that goes to the best American college player each year. Flash and I didn't win it because we played for the Northup Kodiaks in Canada. But Painless deserved it, even though all those American quarterbacks and other offensive players whined that it should have gone to them.

Painless, you see, is a badass. He hits guys with his helmet as he slams into them, and he slams into them as hard as he can. Then it's lights out for his victim, and maybe a trip to the ER to check for broken bones or concussions.

I once asked Flash how the fuck Painless could pulverize opponents that way, game after game, and still come back, looking for more.

"It's what he was born to do," said Flash.

We don't know Painless or the other stuck-up Stars very well. Most of them live on the U.S. East Coast, and most of us Invaders live on the West Coast. We see Painless whenever we're in the same city but seldom say more than hi. I guess he's a decent enough guy when not in uniform and trying to inflict career-ending injuries on opponents.

It's easy for me to feel that our two teams rarely play each other. Those preseason games are ludicrous; they're intended to showcase the rookies and questionable players only. The regular players just sit on the bench. Maybe, in the future, the first-string players will suit up only if the games happen in fun places like Rome, Paris or London.

When we had a preseason game against the stuck-up Stars, I saw Painless before the game and told him that I would play very little that day. "I think I'm going to have some minor orthopedic problems this afternoon."

Painless nodded. "I feel a cold coming on."

I mentioned that most of our first string had suddenly come down with a severe case of the football flu.

"Same with us," he said, grinning. "Something's going around."

The Super Bowl is as far from an exhibition game as there is, and practically every player on both teams would participate in it unless his doctor said no.

Predictably, the sports media are having fun speculating on what will happen when Painless and I collide, or when Flash tries to elude him.

Yesterday, some clown who writes a sports blog quoted Painless as saying that the Invaders didn't really belong in the Super Bowl, anyway, and that the Vegas betting boys needed to be ready for a very lopsided game.

"I hope the Invaders will be ready to learn about football, because we're going to teach them some lessons," the quote said.

I do my best not to be offended by what I read about myself or the Invaders, online or anywhere else. But anyone who claims to ignore the online or on-air remarks about himself is simply lying like a president or prime minister.

So Flash responded to Painless through the sports media this morning, reminding the world of Painless' middle name, Piwi. "With a name like that," Flash said, "it's pretty hard to take that guy seriously as a badass."

A sports reporter asked if Flash might do things a bit differently around Painless.

"I may fake him out here and there."

The reporter reminded Flash that nobody is considered capable of faking out Painless.

"Watch me," replied Flash. "How do you think I got my nickname, anyway?"

I read his words and said, "Flash, if you keep talking that kind of shit, Painless is going to take it all out on me."

"Then *you* can be the one who humiliates him in front of everyone in Great Elizabeth Place."

Francesca Roff asked if we were both so terribly preoccupied with this big black man everyone called Painless.

"Just a little bit," said Flash.

Time for me to take a break. I need to go to Northup University for a practice session with the Invaders. Then I have interviews back at the Hotel Bayporte, where the sports media have overtaken an entire section of a banquet room. Some pushy chick from a women's magazine wants to do an "in depth" piece on me and publish it if we beat the stuck-up Stars. She said she wanted to "hang out" with me and "figure out what makes Reggie run." Flash and I have to do an interview at a downtown TV studio, then hurry back to the Hotel Bayporte for a cocktail party *Canadian Sports* magazine is hosting.

Players loathe those cocktail parties but the owners want us to attend. They think it's good for the NFL that some of us guys show up and talk to the moneyed dummies who want to meet us.

Most of the people who go to those parties are nerdy guys who get drunk and start kissing the asses of the athletes who have the sports careers the nerdy guys have always wanted.

Sheri Rawson and Francesca Roff are bugging Flash and me to take them to dinner at Panache tonight. Francesca wants to go there because she's convinced some celebrities will be there. Panache is Bayporte's only restaurant with any sort of international restaurant. Presidents and prime ministers have eaten there.

I'm fine with Panache. I know we can get a good table, no matter how crowded it is; Flash and I have overtipped Kaj, its owner and manager, enough times when he was just another solicitous, ambitious waiter.

I *do* hope there will be some famous faces at Panache, and I want them to ogle our women, Sheri and Francesca. Francesca's nighttime attire is mostly just underwear, belts and boots. Sheri calls it Francesca's "fuck me quick" outfit.

Catch you later.

Sheri said that she had read my stuff while Flash and I were practicing at the U. and she hoped that Snoop would feel free to polish my words so that I wouldn't seem like an illiterate simpleton from Canada.

I told Sheri I felt quite proud of my book so far, and that I hoped the rest of it would be every bit as good as what I had already written.

I added that Snoop Kowalski seemed hardly the world's greatest collaborator or editor; after all, he was just the boss of the Bayporte *Sun*'s online sports department. His job with me is just to nag me to finish writing the manuscript and make sure I don't misspell my own name. Unfortunately, he's too busy to hang out with me and observe things I would probably miss.

I also explained to Sheri that if Snoop started diddling around too much with what I had written, he would have difficulty doing his job with two broken thumbs. I really don't know much about Snoop's job as Bayporte's premier sports reporter, except that he doesn't like it so much anymore since the news services stopped buying paper and started doing nearly everything online. He says he's a writer, not a Web designer.

I asked about his wife, Jaylene. A successful book collaboration with me would bring him some extra cash to make Jaylene happy. He could buy her whatever fat wives want.

Jaylene, formerly a passably pretty girl named Clarkson, wanted to get married so she wouldn't have to look after herself. She seemed to have the attitude, 'Once I get married, I won't have to worry about looking good. I can be fat and lazy, and there'll be a man to look after me.' She loved to dance and had a big butt and respectable breasts. She smoked Player's Lights, drank Canadian Comfort and said "shit" frequently. Raylene had that slutty look that many men find seductive.

Not that Snoop needs me to toot his horn, but he knows as much about football as any ESPN commentator. Alas, I don't think he'll ever write anything for Sports Illustrated. He's queried them often enough, of course, but they keep declining his submissions, saying they're "unsuitable."

The last time they turned him down, he got so angry that he emailed them, "If you ever decide to stop being a collection of ads for Rolex and BMW and start being a serious sports magazine, contact me and I will work with you."

I told Sheri that Snoop, with his encyclopedic knowledge of football, would be a much better helper on my project than some snob with a master's degree in English from Yale.

"How old is Snoop now?" she asked.

"Not getting any younger," I said. "He covered us all the time when Flash and I played for the Kodiaks. He gave us so much publicity that we were already famous by the time we had graduated." I smiled. "He's a good man."

"I bet he still tries to seduce every Northup coed who interns for him."

"They all think he's a celebrity who knows all the right people and can get those college girls started on big-time broadcasting careers," I said.

I told Sheri that she should try to be more positive when evaluating my manuscript.

She laughed. "Do you remember those porn magazines you and Flash used to show me when we were kids? They totally grossed me out and made me decide never to visit nor become a gynecologist. Well., your manuscript is better than that."

"Fuck you very much," I retorted.

About last night: What can I tell you except that I found the *Canadian Sports* cocktail party exhausting? The Invaders attended but the Stars did not, probably because the Stars are still angry over not appearing on the cover of that magazine although the Invaders did. They even snubbed Painless.

While *Canadian Sports* is hardly even the poor man's *Sports Illustrated*, it is, more or less, Canada's official sports magazine, and the Stars were right to resent not making that magazine's cover. Flash and I have been in *CS* an embarrassing number of times.

The funniest thing about that party was the drunken goof who went up to Flash. The party was full of people I did not know, and that goof seemed to be some abrasive ass from Toronto who had been following the stuck-up Stars since Day One and therefore disliked all Invaders and their fans.

So, this goof approaches Flash and wants to know how Flash will feel when Painless keeps him out of the end zone on Super Bowl Sunday.

Flash laughed at first, thinking that this goof was some practical joker our friends had sent over. Our teammates and friends are always razzing us about something, so we just razz back.

But this particular guy meant business, and we didn't much care for his bellicose tone.

"Wilbert 'Flash' Gortton," the goof said. "Superstar. Big fuckin' deal, eh?"

Flash just stood his ground, with a glass of Canadian Comfort in his hand. He ran his hand through his floppy hair, as he always does.

Their conversation went very much like this:

"Wilbert 'Flash' Gortton," the goof said. "Superstar."

"Speaking," said Flash.

"I want to ask you something, superstar. What would you be doing for a living if you weren't running around catching a football? Have you thought about it?"

"Occasionally I've thought about it," Flash said.

"Tell me about it, superstar," said the goof.

"I thought I might go into mining and minerals."

"Mining and minerals, eh?" asked the goof. "What kind of minerals and mining, superstar?"

"Gold, platinum and diamonds," said Flash. "I've heard they're best kinds of things if you're interested in minerals and mining."

The goof just stared, dumbfounded.

"You understand," Flash said, "that I'm only kidding about mining and minerals. Right now, I have other things I'm doing right now. The mining and minerals can wait till later."

We all stood there, sipping at our drinks.

"It pleases me," said the goof, "that a superstar such as yourself has given some thought to his future occupational opportunities."

"I'm always looking ahead," said Flash.

"No," said the goof, glowering. "You've spent your whole life running into the end zone."

"Only when I had the ball," Flash said.

"You just run around in that dumb uniform and catch a bloody football. Big fucking superstar. For the Invaders! God!"

"Yes, most of the catches I make are for the Invaders," said Flash.

"If it wasn't for the NFL, most of you football faggots would be working in gas stations in the Prairies," the goof

said. "I agree," Flash said.

"You do?" the goof asked.

"Yes, we would be underpaid and overworked. All of us football faggots."

I told the goof that football faggots like us needed to get our beauty sleep, so we were about to return to our hotel.

"Gee, superstar," said the goof, "I hope you do better at Great

Elizabeth Place on Sunday than you've done here tonight."

"Do you have a ticket for the game?" Flash asked.

"Of course. Do you think I flew all the way out here from Toronto just to sit in a hotel room and watch the Super Bowl?"

"Toronto, eh?" Flash's voice sounded loud. "Anyone else from Toronto?"

"Best bloody city there ever was, Toronto," said the goof.

"The people here in Bayporte say that about their city," Flash told him.

"Bayporte sucks, Toronto rocks," the goof said.

"Montrealers think their city is the best place to be," Flash said.

"I'm from Toronto, superstar. Home of the Toronto Stars, the Toronto Blue Jays, the Toronto Raptors." "The

stuck-up Toronto Stars," said Flash. "Great

fucking city, Toronto," said the goof.

"They tell me that the definition of the perfect Toronto woman is that she is about three feet tall, with no teeth and a flat head so you can rest your drink. Is that so?" Flash chuckled.

"Center of the bloody universe, Toronto," said the goof. "They brag about Bayporte, or the West Coast. California, for fuck's sake.

What's California? Just a bunch of nuts, fruits and flakes."

"Yeah, Toronto is sure better than a bunch of nuts, fruits and flakes," Flash said. "It's the flakes I worry about. The nuts and fruits are OK, but those flakes? Bad news, man."

"I want to tell you something, superstar." The goof looked long and hard at Flash.

"Talk."

"You're completely full of bullshit," said the goof. "But you know what? You're one handsome goddamn bastard."

The goof was right: Flash *is* a handsome man.

"You're a smartmouth bloody asshole but you're a goddamn handsome bastard," the goof said.

"It's nice to be appreciated," Flash said.

"Glad my old lady's at home. She'd be creaming in her pants over you," said the goof.

"You shouldn't say that about Ida. She's a very nice woman and she's good to her man," said Flash.

"My wife's name is Margaret, superstar," said the guy. "And you wouldn't like her, anyway."

"I don't think it's very nice of you to speak of Ida that way," said

Flash.

"Who's Ida?"

"Look, guy, we really need to be going. It's been fabulous talking to you," Flash said. He took Sheri's arm and I took Francesca's and we moved toward the exit.

"Good luck, superstar," said the goof. "Just make sure Jethro Pain don't knock your dick in the dirt."

"We'll talk again," Flash said.

"Get lost, you football faggot," said the

guy. "Tell Esther I said hi," Flash told him.

"Her name's Margaret, you retard."

"Say hi to Margaret, too," said Flash.

"The Bayporte Invaders are football faggots," said the goof.

Flash laughed. "God bless the National Football League!"

Upon our return to the Hotel Bayporte, Flash and Sheri started feeling chummy, so they slipped into Flash's bedroom for some quality time together. Sheri kissed me and told Francesca that she and Flash were going into the bedroom to debate about what Emerson meant by "self reliance."

"You and Red better behave yourselves," Sheri said to Francesca.

I switched on the TV and tried to watch a queer tough guy while Francesca lay by my side, gazing at me. I couldn't watch the queer guy while Francesca looked at me that way. I took her into the bedroom and did what the Creator had intended us to do.

I want to add, however, that I could have had a much more fulfilling carnal encounter if Francesca had refrained from asking me a question in the middle of some deeply passionate and sweaty screwing.

"Ees the Super Bowl *really* that important?"

I woke up this morning because Francesca shook my shoulder as she handed me my iPhone. She yawned and blinked, saying that some crazy guy was singing on the phone.

"Jeter Davis," I said, smiling.

I took the iPhone from Francesca and said hello.

I first met Jeter Davis when he was still Manjeet Dhaliwal, one of my teammates on the Northup Kodiaks and a passionate weekend musician. Back then, he didn't have his trademark goatee and denim shirts, nor did he display a surfeit of athletic ability. After graduation and one unmemorable season with the Edmonton Eskimos of the Canadian Football League, he left football altogether and began playing his guitar and writing and singing songs full time, which I considered a wise career choice. He legally changed his name to Jeter Davis, wore jeans and bandanas onstage and had success as a sort of poor man's Bruce Springsteen, playing hurtin' music.

Jeter, like most of my other best friends, was nuts. As unpredictable as a bad wife, he would call me at ungodly hours just to play me a new song.

"Red," he was saying now, "first thing I need to know is the name of that lovely young thing laying beside you. Where does she come from with that funny accent?"

"She's Francesca from Italy," I told him. "At least, that's what she told me. She's also a compulsive liar, so who knows the truth?"

Francesca reached down and pinched my butt. Hard.

"Red," Jeter said, "put her back on the line. I want to serenade her."

I handed the iPhone back to Francesca and leaned over so I could hear as well.

Jeter sang half a dozen of his biggest hits, songs so popular that even Italian girls like Francesca Roff knew them and giggled with recognition.

"Eee's so good," she said, kissing the phone and handing it back to me.

"Jeter," I asked, "are you trying to make time with my main squeeze?" With him, I could never be sure.

"Not right now, Red." He suddenly sounded very serious. "I need to ask you about a matter that means a great deal to me."

"Talk."

"I need to know if the Invaders are going to win on Super Bowl Sunday," Jeter said.

"Gee, I don't know. I think we're gonna lose, man." I paused. "Did you call just to ask me that?"

"Now, Red, you know I'm being serious, so don't jerk me around. I need to know if you Invaders really believe that you can beat those Stars. You've seen the DVDs of them in action. You know what they're good at and bad at. You have inside information that I don't have. I need to have my confidence built up before I can go bet everything I have on you guys. So, do you *really* think you can them on Sunday?"

"The Stars are a hell of a team," I

said. "Oh, Red, come *on...*"

I asked him what the line was in Vegas. Just wondering.

"The Stars are still favored, Red. But not by as much. One of their

black guys got injured. Not Painless."

"The stuck-up Stars don't have injuries," I said. "A Super Bowl

ought to be an even-money bet just because it's a Super Bowl."

"Well, like I said, I need some inside information before I bet big,

and so far you haven't put out," Jeter said.

"Inside information? Don't have any. You know as much about

the stuck-up Stars as I do," I told Jeter.

"Red, no bullshit, OK? I just want to know which of the Stars is a

closet pedophile or has AIDS or is wanted by the cops. You

understand."

"You shouldn't gamble," I said. "It's immoral."

"Just talk to me. I want to bet every dime I have and ever will

have, plus I have friends who want to bet big on this Super Bowl, but

I need to know something nobody else knows. Are you sure you're

going to beat those bloody Stars?"

"Do us another tune, hey?"

"I'm going to do you my latest song."

Francesca and I listened, our long limbs intertwined. Jeter was smart to have switched from football to music. His guitar sounded good; his voice, deep and soulful. Jeter's girlfriends had told him to fuck off enough times that the hurt in his voice was authentic.

"Doesn't that song make you want to jump off a bridge?" he asked.

"Just too tragic. It'll sell a million," I replied. "Say, where are you? Seattle? San Diego? Dallas? Miami?"

"One of those places. Just in a hotel room. They all look the same to me."

"This is a long-distance call, Jeter. I'd like to know where you are. Maybe you could open the window a bit and look outside…?"

"I'm in a downtown hotel in some heartless city," Jeter said. "Outside, it's just a bunch of police cars, office buildings, prostitutes and other nasty people."

"The police would protect you from the prostitutes and other nasty people," I pointed out.

"Would not. The prostitutes and nasty people bribe the cops to leave them alone."

"Jeter," I said, "I have to get up early for meetings. We better say goodnight."

"One more thing, Red. I'm going to be out your way this weekend."

"What?"

"Wouldn't miss it. I've rented a house for the weekend out in West Shore, not far from where you live. I'm going to throw a Super Bowl party on Saturday night. Plenty of barbecued ribs, steaks, booze, you name it. Plus some horny little cuties that's just dying to meet you."

"Jeter, this is the biggest, busiest weekend of our lives. We can't party on Saturday night and then play football on Super Bowl Sunday."

"Be sure you tell Flash and L.T. about it. Maybe they'll be interested."

"No way in hell are we gonna party the night before our biggest game ever."

"You can come by for a steak and a drink and say hi to some nice people. That's not gonna kill you."

"If we showed up, we'd do more than that. Don't wanna play in the Super Bowl with a hangover. Sorry."

"I'll be expecting you, Red. Tell Flash and L.T., all

right?" "Yeah, I'll tell them. Gotta go, Jeter."

"Red, just tell me one more time that you guys can beat those

damn-ass Stars on Sunday."

"We'll beat them, Jeter. We'll kick their asses from one end of

Great Elizabeth Place to the other."

Jeter hooted. "Yeah! I knew it! I'm gonna win a fortune on my

bets!"

"Say goodnight to my Italian sex goddess," I said, handing the

iPhone to Francesca. Jeter said something to her, she blushed and

hung up.

"Eee bet on de Super Bowl, yes?" Francesca asked. "Eees eet so

important to him?"

I pulled her on top of me and said, "You talk too much."

NFL Commissioner Gabe Roder called to wish me luck in the big

game. He added that he had just called the Stars' captain and wished

him luck, too. Roder wanted to remind us to make sure we attended

the Friday luncheon at Great Elizabeth Place.

At that luncheon, every player is supposed to meet premiers, senators, retired military leaders and movie stars. We're also supposed to receive armloads of gifts worth getting, like watches and wallets and silk ties.

I am the Invaders' captain, but some think Vernon Braithwaite, our quarterback, should have that title, or Flash Gortton. Mike Cox, the Stars' quarterback, is their captain.

"You better get Cox back on the phone," I said to Roder, "and tell him we're going to thrash his ass on Sunday."

He laughed. He's an OK guy who's done his best to help us players extract as much money as possible from the teams' owners, most of whom are spoiled brats who want everything to go their way.

Commissioner Roder is also a down-to-earth human being who likes a Canadian Comfort over ice once in a while. He also likes Bayporte, and when he ends up in our town he's not shy about dropping by to say hi, especially when he knows that we've got some Canadian Airways flight attends over who might like to meet a distinguished gentleman such as himself.

It seems to me that trying to write a very personal and truthful book while preparing for the Super Bowl is tantamount to being the last guy in line when a girl is giving out French kisses.

At times, I enjoy these sessions because they allow me to think about someone other than Jethro Painless. Those are the times that I find most gratifying.

Other parts are more difficult, such as providing details, going in-depth and explaining things that bore me. But Snoop Kowalski says that a biographical book must have information that I would rather not include because it's just too tedious to write about.

So I've been typing away about what I did last night and this morning, and have scarcely mentioned Eddie Lowelling, our head coach, or Flash Gortton or Sheri Rawson.

At this moment, Flash is in his huge bedroom, snoozing away a few hours or reading his iPad. He loves those huge European novels he can download for free. Sheri has gone off somewhere to meet up with advertising or fashion people.

Sheri, to the extent that she has a profession, is a model. She is highly in demand as the TV or billboard girl every guy wants to screw and every girl wants to be. For the past couple of years she's been the

Canadian Airways "Won't You Join Me?" girl, licking her lips at the camera.

Byrnes and Jones, the huge Bayporte advertising agency, did all of the campaigns featuring Sheri. Art Jones, the agency's co-founder, accompanied her to some of the shoots and tried to seduce her. Art, like everyone else in Sheri's world, believes that she is Flash Gortton's lover, but that hardly stops him from pursuing her when Flash is elsewhere. Flash and I think it's amusing.

Personally, I think everyone who has ever met her has fallen in love with Sheri. Of course, she loves only Flash, and often me, albeit in a different way.

Sheri stayed in Bayporte because we did, and we remained here because we signed with the Invaders straight out of Northup. We all felt thrilled to be able to stay here, our little family intact.

The Invaders told me beforehand how eager they were to draft me, and I knew they had the first draft pick overall. I replied that I would be delighted to become an Invader—if they would sign Flash Gortton as well. We had decided to remain teammates, even if that meant playing for the Ottawa Rough Riders or Saskatchewan Roughriders.

Bayporte worked out a deal with Miami whereby the Dolphins would draft Flash and deal him to the Invaders in exchange for other players and cash. The Invaders went to some trouble just for Flash and me.

Sheri had given very little thought to her future when Flash and I signed with the Invaders. She simply wanted us to continue as a *menage a trois*, if that's what we were, and she believed that our graduation from Northup should bring out only the most trivial changes in our lives.

As soon as she received her art history degree and knew that she, Flash and I were going to stay in Bayporte, she went into the downtown offices of the Northern Broadcasting System and applied for a job. "I'll answer phones, make coffee. Do you need a secretary or receptionist?"

A producer wandered in from another office, saw Sheri and said, "You're hired! By the way, do you speak English?"

She just made that kind of impression on people. She could have gone into any building in Bayporte or elsewhere and gotten a job. With her beauty and charisma, she made people fear that if she walked out the door, they would never see her again.

Her main duty at NBS seemed to be taking three-hour lunch breaks at Ed Johnson's, a downtown restaurant with many big-screen TVs featuring jai alai matches if nothing else is available. Locals congregate there daily to debate the merits of the city's big-time sports franchises: the Invaders, the NHL Bullies and NBA Rainmakers.

In Ed Johnson's one afternoon, Art Jones saw Sheri and knew at once that he had to sign her up for his agency. He walked up to her and said, his erection obvious, and said, "I'd like to get something straight between us."

Once Sheri stopped laughing, he escorted her back to his office and registered her as his newest model. "Give her our best accounts," he told his creative people. "I want her to be the Canadian Elle MacPherson. Even bigger, if possible."

At first, even though he knew Sheri shared her life with two live-in boyfriends, Art went to some trouble to think of reasons he and she needed to have dinner or cocktails together.

Myself, I think he had just enjoyed putting on his Brioni suits and showing up at exclusive nightclubs and restaurants with a gorgeous woman on his arm. It's not just in Bayporte, either. Art has taken

Sheri to New York, ostensibly on business, and gotten tables at Elaine's and the Beatrice Inn while people like Brad Pitt and Drew Barrymore had to wait.

Sheri, too, has a sense of humor about Art. When Flash and I were in Manhattan during the regular season, she flew out there with Art to hook up with us for the weekend. Sheri enjoyed the admiring glances from all those New Yorkers, who surely wondered why three men were sharing one woman.

"Art is just lonely," Sheri said. "He's trying to be my friend."

"Art is having a big midlife crisis," said Flash. "He likes people to see him with you because they think he's still virile enough to get someone like you."

Well, I can make fun of Art Jones, but check this out: one night in Manhattan, he took Sheri, Flash and me to the Beatrice Inn, and the place as usual was filled to bursting with sensitive artists and snotty club kids who have rich parents but little motivation.

Art pulled the manager aside and said that he needed a table *tout de suite*. The manager nodded, went up to a tableful of garrulous patrons and told them all to get lost.

Art personally seated Sheri as Flash and I pulled out chairs for ourselves. As soon as the server took our orders, Art said, "You see what happens when you party with me? *Do you?*"

So maybe Sheri has gone off to meet up with Art Jones and some other advertising dummies. Flash is napping or reading, so now I'm thinking about our head coach, Eddie Lowelling.

One of the things that Americans don't like about the Bayporte Invaders' involvement in the Super Bowl is that Eddie Lowelling is our on-field boss. He's a tall, corpulent, Mexican-looking guy who worked as the organization's head scout when it was still the Detroit Lions. When the sale went through to Jack Piros, the Bayporte software entrepreneur, all the Lions coaches quit except for Lowelling.

"Eddie's our new head coach," Piros told the world at press conference in downtown Bayporte. "We don't need anyone else. Eddie has the most experience and the best attitude of anyone." Eddie also had the lowest price tag.

How does one describe Eddie? He's a slow-talking Midwesterner who always appears calm. When we were in New Orleans, losing in a game we should have easily dominated, we traipsed back to the locker room and discovered Eddie at the writing board, looking at the felt pen in his hand, as if the pen, and maybe his hand, had just been invented.

Everyone started complaining, softly or loudly, about the weather, the football or the referees. By and by we all settled down and stared at Eddie.

"Well, gennelman," he said at last, "seems plenny of you took a nap out there and that's why we're behind now."

Pol Pott said, "Coach, they're tryin to fake us out. While I got my hands busy with one guy, another guy is gettin past me and gettin to the quarterback."

"That so?" asked Eddie.

"I think we can take these guys," Pol said. "Got lots of football left to play."

"Only way we're gonna win," said Eddie, "is if we stop nappin and start playin football."

"But what am I gonna do about this guy that's always gettin past me?" Pol Pot asked.

Eddie thought for several moments and said, "I got a great idea, Pol. You just get out there and make sure you block your man. If another man gets past you, he's somebody else's problem."

Eddie said he wanted to intensify our passing and pushing games for the second half in order to get some more points on the scoreboard. "I don't believe Flash and Red have had a chance to play enough this game," he said.

We went back out there and won the game. Vernon Braithwaite threw two touchdown passes to Flash, our defense forced two turnovers he converted into field goals, and then Eddie instructed Doc just to hand the ball to me. I rushed for over a hundred yards and scored one touchdown. By the end of the game, I felt so exhausted I feared collapsing on the field.

"Hell of an effort, Red," Eddie said, putting his hand on my helmet. "That's what I like to see."

Eddie Lowelling himself had an outstanding career as a linebacker. He talked to himself, slapped his helmet and generally convinced everyone that he was mentally unstable. People said, "Eddie's not crazy. He's just from Missouri. They all act like that."

In the time I have known him, Eddie has yet to smile. Maybe all those years of looking grim have paralyzed his facial muscles. Or perhaps on Sunday, if we win, he will make a point of smiling for the cameras.

A person would think that Eddie might smile because the Invaders are undefeated, adored by many and reviled by others. Eddie thinks it's nice to have some foes and critics who wish you'd drop dead. "A man without enemies is a man who just hasn't tried hard enough," he would say.

As head coach of the Bayporte Invaders, Eddie deserves plenty of credit for being straightforward and honest with us. He isn't a compulsive liar, like many other coaches. He had everyone's respect last year, when we had a number of injuries, lost games against wimpy opponents and were lucky to finish the season just over five hundred.

Flash says Eddie is the best head coach we could have, and Flash is cerebral about this game. "Winning always happens to the team that wants it more," he says.

Flash has studied this matter with some seriousness and believes that in the NFL, coaches matter less than they do in college football. In college, he says, the players are still kids, naïve and gullible, and will often believe the motivational bullshit the coaches spew at them.

"In the NFL, it's different," Flash says. "We're all good, and we know it. Those pep talks don't mean much to us. We win or lose because of little things that are mostly beyond our control."

Flash says that in the NFL, the winning teams are the ones that stay mentally disciplined throughout the season.

When he says such things, I tell him he sounds like Vince Lombardi, or maybe George Patton.

"Football is mainly just acting like a Neanderthal," he says. "You hit and get it, chasing after the ball. Once in a while, all of the elements come together, and you have a winning team.

"Maybe that's the definition of a winning team: a bunch of guys who find losing totally unacceptable. Of course, everybody wants to win, but that's not the same thing as saying *I cannot accept failure*. The guys who think that way end up in the Hall of Fame."

We had a meeting this morning, and Flash did some talking.

"We refuse to lose this Super Bowl to those stuck-up Stars. There will be moments out there when we play even better than we thought we could, and that's because we'll be playing as a team, not just as a bunch of guys wearing identical clothing."

The only thing Eddie Lowelling said at that meeting was that our workout would be the usual thing, and he added that afterwards we would have a photo opportunity "with some local cuties that's just dyin' to meet ya."

I remember hoping that they wouldn't let L.T. get too close to those cuties.

Hello, world, this is Red Crossley. back at the MacBook Pro. I'm all prettied up and ready to do some serious writing about things and stuff. Flash, Sheri, Pol Pott and Pol's wife have gone off to dinner to eat and listen to some live music. I declined to join them because I find music while I eat is a nuisance, unless it's Jeter Davis who's singing, but it's been some time since Jeter has been needy enough to sing at a restaurant. Also, I feel the desire to write, and I may not feel this way later.

I told Sheri to take her iPhone along and call me when they're done eating, and I might hook up with them a bit later for a couple of Canadian Comforts over ice. I ordered up a steak sandwich, fries, coleslaw and a pot of coffee for dinner, and now I'm going to write about Wilbert "Flash" Gortton.

I think I've made myself pretty clear that I believe Flash is the best wide receiver in NFL history, and he makes life vastly easier and better for Vernon Braithwaite, who I believe is the best quarterback since Joe Montana and Troy Aikman.

Even the most brainless of sportswriters—and that includes most of them—acknowledge that Flash is probably even better than Jerry Rice.

What makes Flash so great? His hands seem slathered with glue, his concentration is unwavering, he has so much stamina that I sometimes wonder if he has a third lung, he is as fast as a leopard and runs all routes perfectly. Most fans think that all great receivers share these qualities, but not so. Flash is unique.

As I've said, he is a very handsome man. His blond hair flops about in brass-colored ringlets, and he's got these big blue eyes like a three-year-old. But he's also got this body by Nautilus, and the whole package of Flash just makes women lick their lips like they could eat him with a spoon.

For me, Flash is the best friend I've ever had, and the brother I've never had. He and Sheri have always been the family I've always wanted, which is why I have gone to some trouble to keep the three of us together. People scratch their heads at Red Crossley, treating his friends Flash and Sheri like kin, but to me they are just that.

But don't feel sorry for me. I have more love around me each day than most other people have in an entire year. I always have. Flash's parents have always treated me as a second son, and Sheri's folks have always kept an eye out for me. There was also my Uncle Andy, who did his best to be a surrogate father to me.

The social workers have an expression, 'broken home.' That really sums up my situation as a child. My father ran away during my infancy. He fixed cars during the day and stole them at night.

My mum served meals at some restaurant and entertained her high-tipping customers after work. That left Uncle Andy, a professional gambler and boyfriend to many girls.

Inevitably, kids grow up, and they become whomever they choose to be. Their choice is always influenced by the friends they have acquired.

Fortunately, I had Uncle Andy. He spent time with me and took me to all the sports events I wanted to see. He also taught me plenty about gambling and people and life in general.

Uncle Andy said, "If you like sports and gambling, you'll learn about how to get along with others and you won't ever end up in prison."

Flash and I had great fun just hanging out together. Each day brought an adventure. We laughed about everything, even the really bad things that happened occasionally, things worse than losing the provincial football championship.

What could be worse than losing a huge football game? Losing Flash's mum one awful afternoon.

His birth mother—not his stepmother, who entered his life not terribly long after his real mother's funeral—was killed trying to cross the street on a typically abysmal Bayporte autumn afternoon. She hurried across the roadway, but an oncoming car with a distracted driver shore off her leg. Through some miracle, the ambulance arrived and transported what was left of her to Bayporte General Hospital, where surgeons sewed her up in time. She remained in a coma for a day or two, and died while Flash and I, after close to an hour of staring at her, decided to slip away for a few minutes to get a couple of pops from the machine down the hallway.

Mr. Gortton had done a good job of preparing Flash for his mum's death, and when it happened, he hugged his father, grandmother and aunt, then said, "I need to be alone for a while." He meant that he needed to be alone with Sheri and me, so we three headed out to Paul's Submarine Stop, where we did our most intense and profound thinking and talking.

On our way to Paul's, Flash said something that so mystified me that I didn't think I had heard him right.

He said, "At least now I won't have to eat any more lima beans." I grunted, to tell him that I had heard him.

"I've been trying to think of something good that's come out of my mum's death," Flash said. "And now I know what it is: I'll never have to eat another lima bean. She put those nasty little fuckers on my plate three times per week. Well, no more of *that* bullshit."

He has always been able to find humor in things. People, to him, are the funniest things of all. Flash can imitate people with eerie accuracy after observing them for a few minutes.

Even now, he can imitate Lord Larry Rawson, Sheri's dad, so well that Sheri and I howl with laughter.

Lord Larry Rawson made his money in the "mining and minerals business," as he would say. Lord Larry speaks often of flying to Ottawa to get "tax breaks from M.P.s who know nothing about mining and minerals." He tells us about "major excavations" in "the

58

ass-freezing Yukon."

Lord Larry is a leading figure in Bayporte, which explains how he became known as "Lord" Larry. Great Elizabeth is a province pleasantly besotted with cultural prizegiving, and some years back our premier honored Larry Rawson, who had put many people to work and stimulated our economy, with the title member of the Order of Gentlemen. Larry could spend the rest of his life signing his name, "Larry Rawson, O.M.," just as knighted Britons added "O.B.E." to their names.

Alas, Larry considered such an honor insufficiently regal, so he decided to call himself Lord Larry and his wife Lady Joy. The local media loved it that this self-important rich guy would give himself and his snooty, vain wife these fake titles. Bayporte needs colorful local people like Lord Larry and Lady Joy. The city, sliced in half by the raging Tyson River, glitters like a new toy due to the constant construction of skyscrapers. In Bayporte, old equals ugly.

The constant construction, a result of Canada's vast natural resources and her relatively few mouths to feed, does nothing, of course, to stop the city's year-round, pelting rain.

My alma mater, Northup University, is a huge collection of redbrick buildings, and, on a gray day with plenty of pallid students milling about, it's easy to pretend that Northup is some very distinguished, very old British liberal arts university. But Northup trains engineers, research scientists, agricultural specialists and athletes; Chaucer-reading eggheads and theatre majors need not apply.

To me, the best feature of Bayporte is its people, who mostly are decent, honorable folks who do their best. I'm told that a sign used to say WHERE THE TRUE NORTH BEGINS, and at one time the place was full of loggers and miners instead of car dealers and travel agents.

Another slogan said TORONTO FOR CULTURE, BAYPORTE FOR FUN, and I have no idea what that hell that was supposed to mean. Maybe they meant that Bayporte could be a fun place for kids with lively imaginations, and that certainly applied to Sheri, Flash and me.

"Why," we asked Sheri, "does a rich guy like your dad live in a place like Bayporte?"

"Because," she answered, "he sort of *owns* it."

Lord Larry confuses me. He has the financial freedom to live anywhere in the world he wants to, but he stays in a city where it rains all the time and the traffic jams get worse every year.

Lord Larry, of course, is a prominent person in Bayporte. He's big in golf, big in West Shore Country Club, where he and Lady Joy hang out. He's a respected man out at Northup, a lifelong Kodiaks fan who paid for extensive stadium renovations after they fired a football coach who annoyed him.

Lord Larry forever flies out to Ottawa for lunch appointments with Members of Parliament who can pass laws that make life better for people like him; then he goes to Toronto, to meet up with the people staffing his eastern office. He goes down to Montana, where he owns a ranch, then out to Washington, D.C., to pester the American bureaucrats. If he has time, he flies down to Puerto Vallarta, too.

He knows everyone of significance in Bayporte banking circles, and he's bragged about the mayors, premiers, governors and other elected officials he has helped. I don't think anyone in this city can do much of anything without Lord Larry's permission.

Lord Larry, of course, is married to Lady Joy, and she is as much a prominent Bayporter as her husband. She has put herself in charge of cultural activities and civic associations; she oversees what the public library and private schools do. Recently, she created "pink days" throughout high schools in which bullied students were to feel free to identify their tormentors. She then called some of the bullies' parents at home and demanded to know why they let their little monsters abuse those other children.

The Rawsons are handsome people. Lord Larry is tall and lean, with a headful of wiry gray hair. He wears dark Brooks Brothers suits that Lady Joy orders for him a dozen at a time. She, too, is tall and slim, artificially blonde and tan, with a white-and-peach wardrobe from *Real Housewives of Beverly Hills* that looks a bit peculiar here in rainy, gray Bayporte. She shows up with some unforgettable hairdos, and owns a number of wigs in case her hairdresser botches up the job. She goes to Boccasio and buys thick, chunky gold jewelry that's so real it looks fake. When Lady Joy goes out, she checks her look in the mirror or every available reflective surface.

As I say, Flash can do a fine impression of Lord Larry. Both men have deep, resonant voices, so it's easy for Flash to fill his lungs with Lord Larry's bombastic tones. Flash especially loves to imitate Lord Larry at a restaurant: "Sweetie, I need a Grade A Alberta tenderloin, medium well."

Sometimes Flash will do Lord Larry at length.

"The thing that irks me today is how many kids there are who simply don't understand what has made Canada the best bloody country in the whole world.

"Canadian is a great country simply because of what we white men have done for it. When we first got here, it was only Natives here who didn't know anything at all about education, progress and all the other things that make life good.

"But the white man arrived and taught the Natives about what civilization was. They learned from us about cleanliness and decency and politeness.

"The white man taught the entire world and gave the world gifts like electricity, aviation, TV and computers and all the rest of the good stuff that the world can't do without now.

"If the white man had failed to take charge of the world and left it up to everybody else, we'd have none of today's advances and probably all kinds of disease and despair and definitely lots of Communism.

"Kids today should admire the white man and ignore the Natives,

Pakis and blacks. Those colored people are good for nothing except smoking crack and having illegitimate children.

"I don't like to brag, but I must say that it's people like me, Lord Larry Rawson, who have made Canada the most admired country in human history. I've put thousands of people to work and paid them what they're worth, and sometimes even more.

"Hard work is the best thing there is. I've worked hard ever since my dad dug up gold and silver he wasn't even looking for. I'm still working hard even though I don't have to. I could sit on my ass all day or just play golf, but I work anyway. I do know how to gave a good time, though. Nothing wrong with that, nothing at all.

"Let me tell you what is wrong with the youth of today. One Paki plus one Native equals drug addiction and Communism. There it is. It's that simple.

"Sweetie, I need a Grade A Alberta tenderloin, cooked medium well."

I had to stop typing to answer my iPhone. Sheri had called to say they were at some restaurant that had a stand-up comic as funny as Jim Carrey and a singer who reminded her of Joni Mitchell.

"We're about to go," Sheri said.

"Then go, but call me again from wherever you end up. I'm writing like a son of a bitch right now. I'm telling the world about your mum and dad."

"Oh, fuck. Did you mention that Mum's ancestors owned some European country centuries ago before their slaves ran them off? Or at least, that's what *she* claims."

"Don't know if I'll be able to remember everything Lady Joy likes to brag about. Say, did she claim to have invented the Internet?"

"Gotta go, babe.. We're thinking of checking out a new place called the Combat Zone.. It's right on Robertson Street, next door to everything else here in downtown Bayporte. It's all changed a bit since we were college pukes, hey?"

"Combat Zone?" I asked. "Never heard of it, but I'm sure I'll find it. I sneak up on you and spray you with napalm in an hour."

"Sounds good," said Sheri. "Now you get back to writing and don't stop till you can't think of anything more to write."

"I'm typing as fast as I can. See ya."

"Red Crossley, you get your homework

done!" "OK. Gotta go."

"Red Crossley, you quit going to the washroom with that nudie magazine!"

"I'm just takin' a shit, Mum. Bye."

I hung up, practically shaking with laughter. Sheri and Flash can often do that to me. Sheri was the first real kidder in my life, and she got us expelled from Oliver Johnson High School when we were fourteen.

The people who ran the school made the colossal scheduling blunder of putting Flash, Sheri and me in the same music class at the same time. When cranky old Mr. McLeod, our instructor, left the classroom for a few minutes, he foolishly put Sheri in charge, mostly because she was beautiful, musically gifted and the object of his infatuation.

He asked her to stand in his place and lead us in singing until he returned, and she made sure all was business as usual for a couple of songs until Wilbert "Flash" Tiller raised his hand.

"Yes, Wilbert?" Sheri asked with phony impatience.

"Miz Rawson, I was just wondering if we could stop singing this goofy shit?"

Everyone laughed, including Sheri.

"We'll sing whatever you want," Sheri said, "as long as you and Mister Crossley here get up and sing, too."

So, within a minute, Flash, Sheri and I stood before the class. The song Flash chose, *Casey Jones*, had some of the raunchiest lyrics ever written. Marines sang it often on their mile runs.

One thing: Our principal was named Keith Carlson Jones, and everyone called him K.C. Jones. So one could construe our song as being about him.

> *K.C. Jones was a son of a bitch*
>
> *Drove his train in a thirty-foot ditch*
>
> *Came on out with his dick in his hand*
>
> *Said, "Listen, ladies, I'm a hell of a man"*

There was more, much more of it. We sang it loudly and passionately, and we got through all the lyrics twice. When we finally shut up, we looked to see our doorway filled with Mr. Jones' glowering, shaking person.

We sat in Mr. Jones' office for over an hour until Lord Larry arrived to rescue us.

Mr. Jones sat at his desk, breathing hard and staring red-faced at some documents as we sat opposite him, not really knowing where to look.

Mr. Jones squinted up at Sheri and said, "Miss Rawson, you realize, of course, that this incident will disqualify you from being elected to student government."

Flash said, "But, sir, that means the world to her!"

Sheri had to fight to keep from bursting into peals of laughter.

"As for you," Mr. Jones said to me, "I really don't hold you personally responsible. If Rawson and Gortton decided to jump off the Tyson River Bridge, the recovery crew would find your body clinging to theirs."

"Thank you, sir."

Just then, Lord Larry arrived and insisted that we remain seated so we could hear what the two men had to say to each other concerning our infraction.

"I feel I can speak to everyone about everything, no matter what it is. I refuse to say, 'You young people need to leave this room while we adults speak to each other,' " Lord Larry said.

"As you wish," said Mr. Jones.

"Now, Keith, we need to remember when we were kids and did

things sometimes that were regrettable. Back then, there was some grownup who gave us a second chance on the condition that we promised never to do those stupid things again. Right now I'm concerned about my daughter and these two nice, decent young fellows whom I have known for most of their lives."

"I can see that you feel strongly about his matter," said Mr. Jones.

"Keith, I know that you're feeling very offended by what has gone down today, and you probably want to toss them out of this school and be done with them. But let's not act rashly.

"What would you lose if you expelled the three of them? I'll tell you: First, you would lose a future class president who in the next few years will distinguish herself in a dozen ways at this school. You would also lose two boys who have already demonstrated superior athletic ability."

Mr. Jones shrugged. "Their transgressions are so reprehensible that I should expel them and force them to repeat this year in the fall."

Lord Larry frowned. "Keith, I really do think we should give more thought to the consequences of that kind of discipline. If you expelled them or failed them, they would fall behind and become the laughingstocks of the school. The next thing you know, they would become street kids, or get mixed up with drugs and Communism."

Mr. Jones just stared at him.

"Keith," Lord Larry said, "think about when you were a boy and some of the dumb things *you* might have done."

"You mean like singing profane songs that mock the principal?"

Lord Larry smiled. "Then give some thought as to who Larry Rawson is."

Mr. Jones said he would suspend the three of us for three days, period. Lord Larry shook his hand and marched us out of the office, looking very pleased with himself.

Lord Larry drove all of us to his grand estate in West Shore. The ride in his Rolls Royce was smooth, even enjoyable, until the big man broke the silence by asking, "So, Sheri, what do you think of these two smartasses now that they've gotten you into trouble requiring your father's intervention?"

Sheri said, "I think they have no musical talent at all."

Lord Larry stayed silent, but his face turned many colors.

When we reached the Rawsons' home, he ordered us to sit in the living room, which was bigger than many other people's homes. His living room, dominated by big pieces of furniture, wooden tables and

African art, had a six-foot, flat-screen TV set that made my eyes bug out. Sheri had told me that her dad had framed letters in his den from heads of state and Oscar-winning actors, but I cared only about the cars and TVs and aircraft that only the Rawsons of this world could afford.

Lord Larry said that Lady Joy would be home soon and then we could all sit and have a long talk about what had happened that afternoon. Then he walked out of the room to make a phone call. I think he called Uncle Sam, offering to buy Hawaii.

Sheri said her mother had probably stayed late to supervise the cleanup of the meeting of Women Who Want to Save the World from Itself.

Flash stepped into the hallway—cell phones hadn't been invented yet—and used their other line to call his dad, who owned Gortton's Groceries. He explained that he was at Sheri's house with her and me, and why.

I did my best to eavesdrop and got the impression that Flash's father dismissed it all as a youthful misadventure.

"Yeah, Dad," I heard him say. "We were singing *Casey Jones* while the teacher was out and, you know, the principal has the same bloody name, just spelled differently, so I guess we should have known better. I think he got mad because it was Sheri who sort of started it and her family is rich, you know. Yeah, I'm at her home now. I'll tell them you said hi."

I would have called Uncle Andy about this matter, but I wasn't sure how to reach him and his only concern would have been if Flash and I could continue our high school athletic pursuits.

Lady Joy finally appeared, wearing a white jumpsuit, tan runners and peach-colored plastic glasses.

"So," she said, "a Rawson gets suspended from school for mocking the principal. Very nice. The three of you have made big fools of yourselves today."

"Actually, ma'am," said Flash, "I started the

trouble." "Like hell," Sheri said.

"Doesn't matter started it," said Lord Larry. "I finished it. Saved all three of you from being expelled."

"Thank you for your help, Mr. Rawson," said

Flash. "Same for me," I said.

"My dad says it's too bad Sheri was in on this unfortunate thing," Flash said.

"Your father has a very nice store. I've been in it a few times," said Lady Joy. "I've bought his milk and butter."

"Yes, ma'am. He sells that," said Flash.

"Nice for you, Mum," said Sheri.

"I've bought pop there. It tasted cold and sweet," I said.

"Is Gordon's Groceries still over that way, where the Indians and Pakistanis have all taken over?" asked Lady Joy.

"Mum..." Sheri blushed and rolled her eyes.

"Yes, ma'am. It's still on Fraser Avenue, where it's always been," said Flash.

Lady Joy said, "Sheri, I didn't mean to *offend* anyone by asking Wilbert about his family's store."

"No offense taken, ma'am," said Flash.

"Also, I think our salt and pepper came from Gordon's," Lady Joy said.

Flash nodded. "Yeah, we've got that."

Sheri let out a huge sigh and closed her eyes.

Lord Larry said to Lady Joy, "Sweetie, we had a serious chat at the principal's office and these kids have promised to mind their manners from here on out."

"We'll never live this down at the country club," she said.

"I'm not going to get too excited about that," said Lord Larry.

"Of course you won't. You'll be on a flight back east or down south."

"The people at the country club know better than to talk about me to my face or behind my back," Lord Larry said.

Lady Joy looked away from him and took a drag of her Player's Light. Flash and I exchanged glances, and Sheri just sat there with her eyes closed.

"This really isn't such a big deal," said Lord Larry. "It's nothing beyond the capacities of smart white folks."

"What about dumb colored folks?" asked Sheri.

"Hey?" Lord Larry asked, frowning.

"Just talking to myself."

"Sheri, don't be a smartmouth," said Lady Joy.

"This meeting is adjourned," said Lord Larry. "One of my guys is coming by tonight and we have to see what we're going to do about our Yukon project."

We all got up.

"Tell your father we like his store," said Lady Joy.

"I've met your dad. He's a stand-up guy," said Lord Larry.

"Thank you, sir. I'll tell him you said so," said Flash.

"And how about *you*, Richard? How is your uncle?" asked Lady Joy.

"He keeps busy," I told her.

"He was quite the golfer here some years ago," said Lord Larry. "He was so good that some us thought he should be on the pro tour." He paused. "Well, anyway, boys, you need to behave at school from now on so I don't have to go out there and throw my weight around like I did today. And while you're at it, keep my daughter in line, too."

"Yes, sir," Flash and I answered in unison.

As Flash and I headed out the door, Lord Larry called out to me, "What the hell *is* your uncle doing these days?"

"Everyone he can," I answered.

Lord Larry and Lady Joy laughed, pretending that they got the joke.

"You boys are welcome here whenever you like," said Lady Joy. "Thank you, ma'am," we said. "Be seeing you, Sheri."

We hustled out of the house and across the big front yard, and as we reached the tall iron gate, Flash whirled around and hollered, "Dame Rawson! The next time you are desperate enough for groceries that you go into my family's store, don't worry about all the Pakis who are hanging around outside. Just remember that they're more afraid of you than you are of them!"

We smiled at the sound of Sheri's raucous laughter as we sprinted away. Even as a kid, she had the finest laugh in the world.

Snoop Kowalski insists that I include something in this about the way Flash and I live while we're not playing football, especially about our activities during the off-season.

"Something that reveals your likes, dislikes and values beyond the football field," said Snoop.

Frankly, Snoop, I think you're full of bullshit, but I'll talk about my off-the-field life, if you want me to do so.

As I write these words, I start to resent the notion that people might think a football player is just some overgrown bully who gets paid to get out on the field and injure his opponents.

I want to emphasize that during the off-season Flash and I have the quietest possible lives. We stay in Bayporte unless we have endorsements to honor in Los Angeles. Our off-seasons seem to end too quickly; entirely too soon, training camp starts up again.

During the off-season, we'll agree to go to make a speech at a local luncheon for a thousand-dollar fee. If, as sometimes happen, the sponsor of the event says he can't afford my fee, I stay home. I really don't like those speaking engagements, anyway.

Many star players have second careers they pursue in the off-season so that as soon as they retire from football they'll go full-time into that other career. Flash and I have plenty of money already, so once football is over, we will have many options as to what to do with the rest of our lives. We can just sit and vegetate and never worry about money.

Sometimes a player must travel to big cities and eat rubber-chicken dinners, then get up and make a speech. We do this when they throw so much at us that we can't say no. The sponsors will even make sure the speaker gets laid.

When we manage to get a warm, dry few weeks in Bayporte, Flash and I do as much golfing as we can.

I will confess to one thing: I have often thought that after retiring from football, I would like to open a restaurant or nightclub of some kind.

That would be a good idea, as I say, after I've retired and my body is so beaten up that I can't do much of anything else.

My restaurant would have to be located in Los Angeles, in or near some swanky neighborhood like Westwood or maybe Beverly Hills, so my customers wouldn't have to worry about being stabbed, robbed or shot. We would need a spacious parking lot. We would serve big drinks and big portions and stay open good and late. We would not hire any arrogant pretty boys to wait on tables while they're trying to become actors.

I would encourage young women to become frequent customers by offering them complimentary or very inexpensive cocktails. The dining area would be huge, with big tables and chairs spaced well apart so that conversations and seductions could happen discreetly.

Casual dress only. Jeter Davis' music would fill the restaurant through hidden speakers, and the menu would be filled with goodies like authentic barbecue and many kinds of salad.

I guess I would call it the Fifth Quarter and hang pictures of Flash Gortton all over the walls.

But that's for another day.

Flash has a different set of ideas on how to spend his post-Invaders years. He likes to invest our money in the stock market. "It's the craziest fuckin' game around," he says.

Flash, an astute stock-picker, says that virtually everybody in the financial world is a perfect idiot.

"I have yet to meet a CEO who has the brains to wipe his butt after he drops a deuce," says Flash. He adds, "The only way to get rich is to inherit it, marry a rich person or be so totally incompetent that they kick you upstairs."

We have off-season business dealings and meet with people who have made big impressions on Flash. We've lunched with rich, brainless supporters of the Invaders and we've gone to some of Bayporte's more exclusive hangouts to visit with other cretins.

I suppose we enjoy these outings with mental midgets because we always accept their invitations. Flash, were he not a sports superstar, could have a thriving public-relations career. He's glib, handsome and a snazzy dresser. I think he has more than enough charisma for Hollywood, and he certainly could thrive on Wall Street, considering all the good financial patterns he's run and the bad advice he's ignored.

Our apartment, a penthouse on the southern edge of West Shore, is the very one in which Howard Hughes once camped out for nearly a year in the 1960s. We have a spacious living room and bar, three oversized bedrooms, a kitchen every gourmet chef would envy, and a terrace that looks out for everything worth seeing. Flash has covered it with hardwood floors and the most comfortable furniture around.

We have a state-of-the-art sound system, big-screen plasma TVs and abstract art that Flash bought because you can stare at them all day and never get sick of them. There are also some frame pictures of us, scoring touchdowns and being tackled.

For company, we have a vicious black cast named Oliver. A stray, he darted into the lobby while he had the door open as we entered the building. Impressed by his caginess, he let him move in. He's loud and tough and tries to eat our clothes.

Our apartment is known as the site of unforgettable parties, many planned and others spontaneous. Our teammates come by to find out if we've made friends with any new Canadian Airways flight attendants or if Sheri has any new model friends over.

When we first moved into this building we organized a weekly party and invited a few friends and some of the prettier, higher-class hookers, get drunk and naked, then do what naturally follows. We had famous friends come by while they were in town, enjoy our hospitality and then fly back home to Los Angeles. If I had video recorded what they did during our orgies, I could make a billion dollars blackmailing them.

Now I have to stop typing and head out to meet up with some nice people on Robertson Street, even though I would rather just stay here in my deluxe suite at the Hotel Bayporte and watch TV or eat a hot fudge sundae.

But Flash says, "A man *must* make fun one of his top priorities in life. The life without fun is not worth living." Of course, that's just his way of rationalizing the Canadian Comforts over ice and joints of weed he enjoys in his own fun-filled life.

We may get a bit of that fun tonight, too.

This, therefore, is Red Crossley, telling you that the screen is going dark and the battery blinking red. Time to give this MacBook a rest; I'm off to Combat Zone. Hope they don't card me, because I can't find my driver's license right now. This reminds me of Flash's response when we were underage carousers and bouncers demanded to see proof of our ages.

Flash, looking like a shell-shocked Army veteran with his sunglasses on, khaki jacket zippered up and a cigarette hanging out of his mouth, would say, "They didn't care about my age when I was in Vietnam killing gooks."

PART TWO

CHICKS

Frankly, I'm completely exhausted from last night's fun. I may have to refrain from partying until we've beaten the stuck-up Stars.

That nightclub we went to, Combat Zone, was perfectly adequate if all a man wanted was drinking booze, smoking dope and messing around with wanton women.

Francesca Roff was hardly the sexiest woman there, and even Sheri Rawson didn't place absolutely first. At least, that's how Flash and I saw things, and we saw many things: faces, breasts, bums, vaginas.

Now, if you don't think that's more provocative than Grandpa's underwear, you're reading the wrong book.

Only the Great Coach Up There could have said who these young lovelies were, or why, indeed, He had chosen them to be so irresistible. But they were quite an assortment of magnificent breasts, mile-long legs, big empty eyes and expertly woven hair.

Sheri called them California Girl wannabes.

Those women really had nothing going for them except physical perfection. They just kind of wander around and twirl their woven hair. They get on the floor and do slow dances by themselves, with each other or with swishing homosexuals. They remain silent, but if they do speak, they usually say something like, "Hey! Can you tell me how to get a job as a correspondent for *Entertainment Tonight?*"

We asked the management about these young ladies. We wanted to know who they were and who they hoped to become. But nobody could tell us anything. You just can't get a straight answer from the people who work there.

One of the people we consulted on this matter, Wade Sellers, the TV actor, sat with us, right next to Francesca Roff, delighting Francesca.

"Those girls just want to get next to someone who can get them green cards," Wade said.

My general conclusion was that Combat Zone was a fun place to be, if they could get rid of some of the homosexuals.

At the entrance, we had to walk down a half-flight of steps into a sort of trench. All around, we heard turned-down sounds of explosions, gunfire and urgent commands shouted in what was probably Vietnamese.

Some little gook in a Viet Cong uniform comes up to us and asks if we are members. Then he takes you to foxholes, or whatever they are, in which everyone is sitting on a military trunk. The foxholes are the only seating areas, and everyone in the foxholes looks up at the dance floor and those on it.

Mosquito nets lay draped over virtually everything and the whole place seems camouflaged in yellow and green. Off to one wall, soft lighting highlights a big picture of a serious-looking Vietnamese man in a khaki uniform.

The dance music, and you companions' conversation, are difficult to hear in the foxholes due to the gunfire, explosions and Vietnamese yelling. But on the dance floor, the gunfire and whatnot are inaudible and the music is virtually deafening because the speakers are bolted into the ceiling.

"Combat Zone," I yelled over the din of the piped-in war sounds, "should be called Hash Den or Opium Den." I pinched my nose. "Whew!"

Wade Sellers smiled and lit up a cigarette, sucked on it and passed it around. He took out a second cigarette and repeated the process. The servers, too, took a few hits, which may have compromised the quality of their job performance.

When I first found the table where my friends were, I had to squint through the darkness to figure out who exactly was there. The first person I saw, Wade Sellers, extended his hand as he sat curled up with Francesca Roff. "Nice to meet a fellow jock," he said. "I played a bit back in my college days, too."

I felt like saying that I didn't know Euphoric State had a football team.

Flash sat cuddling Sheri. He said, "This really is a fun place, Red. We should check it out on a regular basis." He gestured up to the dance floor. "See for yourself."

I looked up at the dancers and saw many slim, shapely legs in skirts and dresses. No slacks.

"Yeah," I said. "Nice."

"Look harder, Red," Sheri said. "You're not seeing all there is."

I looked harder, much harder. Then I saw what she meant: the management must have put up a sign saying UNDERWEAR PROHIBITED.

"Just makes you want to sit and stare all night, eh?" Sheri asked, smirking.

I was just about to ask Sheri who I had to fuck to get a Canadian

Comfort over ice in that place, when I suddenly felt something warm and soft by my side, and a soft female voice asking me what I wanted to drink.

"You're Red Crossley, right?" she asked.

"That's me," I said.

"These people said you'd be here."

"They speak the truth," I told her.

"Would you like a drink right now," she asked, "or would you just rather sit here and visit with me?"

"Can't I have a drink *and* a visit?" I asked. "Preferably in that order."

"What'll you have?"

"The only drink worth having. Canadian Comfort over ice."

"I'll be right back."

Our server, Stacey, brought me as many Canadian Comforts over ice as I wanted, and seemed flattered by how I ogled her breasts. At some point I also noticed that Pol Pott and his old lady were there, both of them asleep despite the noisiness of the place.

A man's imagination can run a bit wild when he's sitting in a place like that, looking up at many pantiless women and having a sexy server paying far too much attention to him.

Francesca Roff seemed indifferent to Stacey and me because she was engrossed in conversation with Wade Sellers as he plied her with showbiz gossip.

I should be ashamed to write about what happened after we left Combat Zone. We had one of those freaky scenes we usually reserve for our penthouse apartment near West Shore.

We all staggered back to this deluxe suite Flash and I are sharing at the Hotel Bayporte, where, as the shrinks would say, we started exploring ourselves and each other. Nancy Potts got right into the spirit of our loving after Pol fell asleep again. Wade Sellers sat back and checked us out, although he probably wished he were somewhere else, jerking off to gay porn videos.

Sheri participated, but only with Flash. Still, we all enjoyed looking at her marvelous body. She also kept Francesca from getting angry about Stacey's greediness. Stacey, as we'd all hoped, was a completely uninhibited lover, or at least fucker. She certainly got most of us into the spirit of things, even doing some down-and-dirty stuff with Nancy Potts that Pol would not have liked, had he been awake to see any of it.

I must compliment Nancy on her good manners that evening, especially once Flash got out his kinkier sex toys and scented lubricants. Again, I am so damned glad that Pol was sound asleep.

During one of the more intense moments that evening, Sheri recalled something from long ago. She said she had seen something like this in a beaver magazine we had smuggled into school when we were nine or ten. She wanted to call Mrs. Davis, our teacher, to remind her of it. Mrs. Davis had caught us giggling over the magazine while we were supposed to writing essays or something.

Sheri pointed at an image of a wide-open beaver and said, "Mrs. Davis, I would much rather eat a clam or a taco than *that*." Flash and I laughed so hard that our sides ached for days.

Mrs. Davis herself found Sheri's remark high amusing and didn't report us for having that magazine. She confiscated it and took it home for her own enjoyment.

Anyway, we had a fine time at our deluxe suite. I could go on and on about it, but it would just start to sound like one of those porn videos everyone has already seen.

I know it's getting close to game time because everyone and his as-yet-unborn grandchildren are asking me for tickets that I simply have no way of obtaining.

It is now Thursday, a between practice this morning at Northup University and meetings afterwards, I probably received requests for tickets from half a dozen people. I'll probably get more requests over the next day or so.

Downstairs, in the lobby, restaurants and bars, the Hotel Bayporte is getting very crowded with people who've flown in for Super Bowl Sunday.

Flash and Sheri are down there with Lord Larry and Lady Joy, who are staying in the hotel for the weekend because Lord Larry wants to avoid the huge traffic jams that would make getting from their house to Great Elizabeth Place and back again far more inconvenient than normal. This way, Lord Larry and Lady Joy simply have to walk the two blocks from the hotel to the stadium.

Francesca Roff has gone off to escort Wade Sellers as he makes promotional appearances around town.

Fortunately, all we have to do tonight is attend a cocktail party the Northern Broadcasting System is hosting at this very hotel. Following that, we're having a quiet dinner with Lord Larry and Lady Joy.

Lord Larry doesn't particularly like to stay in a hotel that's maybe two miles from his home, nor does he like to have his routine interrupted in any significant way. He's the kind of man other people go to some lengths to accommodate, so maybe he'll be a bit cranky tonight, seeing how he's had to spend a couple of thousand dollars on a hotel room for the weekend. Still, his team is in the Super Bowl, and the Super Bowl is being played in his city, so that may console him just a tiny bit.

Also, because this is our first Super Bowl, Lord Larry insisted that we join him and Lady Joy for dinner so that he could explain to us how to beat the stuck-up Stars.

Lord Larry, you see, is The World's Greatest Expert on Practically Everything.

I believe that if he had a hundred million dollars or so burning a crater in his pocket, he would buy the Invaders from Jack Piros, the software nerd, and fire Eddie Lowelling. Which, I think, would really be quite a good thing.

Lord Larry is convinced that we've had such a successful season because of all the guidance he has given our team.

Lord Larry's game plan is to figure out how many black guys the other team has, and take it from there.

Flash and I sit doubled up for hours laughing at some of Lord Larry's ideas about what makes a winning football team.

Flash loves to imitate Lord Larry holding forth on our game:

"You see, if the other team has a fast blackie"—to his credit, he was always too polite to use the *n*-word—"you've got to stop him early. Stomp on his foot and try to break one of those little bones in his foot that won't heal up for months.

"If you're in a tight spot and need to gain several yards fast, don't trust a blackie with the ball. They're just too lazy to fight their way through for a few extra yards. It has to do with the way their mums have raised them, whether it's in the States or Africa, they're reared not to try very hard. Maybe the day will come when they will learn to try harder and they've invented a few useful things, like a new piece of mining equipment that works forever and needs no maintenance, they will be worthy of getting the football in a crucial situation and get a first down or even a touchdown. But for now, they are what they are.

"I wouldn't trust a blackie with the football in a do-or-die situation any more than I would trust a Paki to give me a root canal.

"Sweetie, I need a Grade A Alberta tenderloin, well done."

Flash and I have pointed out to Lord Larry that the Invaders have some of the best black players in the NFL.

"I didn't say they were *all* useless," said Lord Larry. "Some of the black Invaders are almost as good as the white Invaders. They should be, too, because they're paid enough."

One of our black teammates has a thriving business in Los Angeles selling lingerie. He's never been married, and people wonder about him behind his back. But he's big and tough, so nobody would ask him to his face if he was queer. Myself, I can't believe he's big, black and gay. It just doesn't add up for me.

Pol Pott is one of my best friends in the world, period. A potential Hall of Famer, he outplays himself every game, and, as for being a friend, if I asked him to kill my enemy, he would reply, "You want that motherfucker stuck or shot?"

Through our considerable business connections, Flash and I helped Pol get a very reasonable deal on a Pepsi-Cola distributorship in Mississippi, where he lives on the off-season. We also got his mum her own frozen-soulfood business, and she's making a small fortune from it.

Pol says we're just ravaged by guilt over oppressing the black man for so many years. "If your consciences didn't bug you so much, you would be much better football players," he's told us.

We just tell Pol to sell crack, become a pimp or hip-hop singer; however black dudes make their money if they're not in pro sports.

Although he isn't black, and this section is supposed to be about black Invaders, I want to write now about our quarterback, Vernon Braithwaite.

Eddie Lowelling says that Vernon Braithwaite is the best quarterback in the NFL. I say he's one of the greatest ever.

It's quite obvious that a football team needs a good quarterback in order to be successful, and during my time with the Invaders, we didn't really accomplish much until we acquired Vernon from the Saints.

We procured Vernon through what one might call trickery and deceit. He became an Invader after the Saints assumed he would be crippled for life because of a motorcycle wipeout in his home state of Oregon. Vernon always goes back to Portland, his hometown, whenever he can, at least partly to check out his dozen or so gas stations located throughout Greater Portland. During one of those trips, he drunkenly crashed his bike not far from one of his gas stations.

The gas station's manager called the number for emergencies, which was the direct line to Jim McMillan, the Saints' general manager.

"Vernon's crashed his bike. He's laying out there on the roadway, not moving," said the gas station manger.

So Jim McMillan called Roger Kettyls, the Invaders' general manager, and asked if he had an adequate quarterback yet. Kettyls said no, so McMillan offered him Vernon Braithwaite in exchange for three draft picks.

Kettyls is sometimes not altogether stupid. He told McMillan he would call him back within minutes. Then Kettyls went online and searched through Facebook, Twitter and everywhere else until he found someone who could provide Vernon Braithwaite's cell phone number. He dialed it on the off chance that someone would answer it and give him some idea of Vernon's condition.

Vernon answered it himself. He sounded very drunk and pissed off that his bike seemed damaged, but he assured Kettyls that he was otherwise OK.

So Kettyls immediately called McMillan and made the trade within minutes, faxing signed documents back and forth.

So that's how we got the best quarterback in the NFL. Vernon, of course, fit in with our organization right away. He's a decent-sized guy with a cannon for an arm. He doesn't like being tackled, so he throws himself to the ground whenever a huge opponent gets too close.

Flash says that if I got traded, he'd go with me or retire. I think that if Vernon Braithwaite went elsewhere, Flash would feel much the same way. That's how highly he regards Vernon. I do, too. We're damned lucky to have him. The stuck-up Stars know it, too, and are in no great hurry to take him on when Super Bowl Sunday arrives.

Go Invaders! Yea!

Francesca Roff came in and said she's getting dressed for the Northern Broadcasting System cocktail party and our dinner with Lord Larry and Lady Joy, so I'm using this time to write these words. She said that half the world was in the hotel's lobby, which meant she recognized half a dozen people from TV or the movies.

She said she saw Roger Kettyls, the Invaders' general manager, down there with his arm around Claudia Knaack, the movie star, both of them beaming at everyone as he introduced her around. Sheri, Lord Larry and Lady Joy sat and observed from their table at the Haida Bar, at one end of the lobby, as people walked up to the Rawsons' table to ask Flash to pose for cell phone pictures. Flash is handsome, clever and hugely charismatic, one of the NFL's best ambassadors and advertisements.

As I type these words, Francesca Roff has entered the room, wearing little more than a smile and blush. Time for me to stop typing and start loving. Later.

Now I'm back from doing other things that just couldn't wait. I washed my hands and face and naughty bits. Everyone else is still asleep; I suppose I'm up this early because game time is closing in and I'm getting psychologically prepared for the big game.

Tomorrow, we will do very besides jog around a bit in our T-shirts and shorts, just to stay limber. We won't even look at any more DVDs of the Stars because, as Eddie Lowelling would say, "It's time to suit up and kick ass."

The media have been full of crap about how the trip out here may have exhausted and demoralized the stuck-up Stars, plus the fact that they will play before partisan crowd in Great Elizabeth Place.

Bullshit, I say. The Stars are a totally together football team. They'll be waiting for us. I have the utmost respect for them, most personally and professionally. In every way, the team has undergone a rebirth since the Mitchell cousins, Lloyd and Jay, acquired the franchise and hired Rudy Sperling as their head coach.

I'm aware that everyone thought the stuck-up Stars would amount to very little, but they had the good sense to play poorly and therefore get top draft picks. They finished dead last in the whole NFL, the Toronto fans booed them for close to an hour at the conclusion of their final game, as the worst of the worst, they got to draft Painless, a player every team coveted.

Following their procurement of Painless, the stuck-up Stars did some wheeling and dealing and beefed up their team with Bobby Schnall and Pat Teel from Chicago. Bobby Schnall, a showoff wide receiver from Michigan, during his first season with the Jets, caught nearly as many touchdown passes as Flash did.

The Chicago Bears mystified many people when they parted with Pat Teel, who gained huge yardage and helped get the Bears into the playoffs. A popular local character in Chicago despite, or because of, his couple of arrests for masturbating in a South Side porn theater, plus that shoplifting incident when he tried to boost some bras and undies from a lingerie store.

He has done an outstanding job for the stuck-up Stars and behaved himself, more or less, in Toronto.

Another guy who makes the stuck-up Stars a formidable opponent is Ralph Stefani, their quarterback. I'm not sure he's a Vernon Braithwaite any more, but he certainly is one of the league's premier quarterbacks.

The media have been calling him "the most underrated quarterback in NFL history," and I think they're more right than wrong. Stefani's played for many teams over the years, none of them half as good as he was.

The stuck-up Stars got him a few years ago and he underwent a personal transformation. Rudy Sperling has sat on Stefani, and that discipline has dome Ralph some good. I'm told that Ralph hasn't gotten into a barroom fight since he arrived in Toronto, and he

102

hasn't stolen a police cruiser lately, either. He's also cut way back on his weekend trips to Atlantic City.

I don't know how to characterize the stuck-up Stars. Many claim that they're rowdies off the gridiron; I do know that they're the cockiest guys around. But I can't claim to know any of them particularly well because they aren't my teammates and they live back east and I seldom socialize with them.

The leader of the whole team, Rudy Sperling, dresses like a pimp, in colorful suits and a wide-brimmed hat. He calls all the plays except for the ones that Stefani can't remember.

Sperling hangs out in downtown Toronto and spends hours at a Yonge Street restaurant called Numero Uno. It is a fancy, popular restaurant when not closed due to bomb threats.

Rudy Sperling is the greatest of friends with the Mitchell cousins, Lloyd and Jay, who own the stuck-up Stars. I've been told that they all grew up together in Toronto. I know that Rudy fixed up the Mitchells with their present wives, Lisa and Karen, who are pretty women even if they are over-the-hill strippers.

I met up with all of them once at Johnny Rogers', a Toronto restaurant for sports freaks, when Sperling and the Mitchells were having a celebratory dinner with Painless, whom they had just signed.

Painless sat sandwiched between the Mitchells' wives, who kept touching his arms as they took turns talking to him, and Rudy Sperling sat with Lloyd and Jay, the three men having a serious pow-wow of their own.

I entered Johnny Rogers' with Flash and Sheri, and as soon as we saw the two Mitchell women with their lacquered hair, pushed-up breasts and real fur coats that looked fake.

Sheri said, "Aw, just a couple of class broads."

We agreed to go over and say hello, and also to congratulate Painless. He shook hands with us and smiled, but the others completely ignored us.

I said, "Congratulations on signing with Toronto. It's a pretty good city."

Jay Mitchell said, "It's the only city worth being in."

Flash, Sheri and I might have stood there a bit longer making small talk with Painless, except that one of the Mitchell women looked vaguely in our direction and said, "I was just thinking how lovely it would be if the three of you weren't here."

We shrugged and walked over to the bar. Sheri said, "I repeat: Just a couple of class broads."

I can hear everyone starting to wake up now. Flash and I have a meeting to attend, then a luncheon, and finally one last workout. A bit later on, I'll fill you in on last night's Northern Broadcasting Service party and our dinner with Lord Larry and Lady Joy. Freakin' funny as all hell.

Right now, it is just after six o'clock on a Friday evening in Bayporte, Great Elizabeth, Canada. In under fifty hours, time will expire on the Super Bowl clock and the Bayporte Invaders will be the NFL champions.

I sit and think about this in my oversized bed in my opulent suite in the Hotel Bayporte, one of the most expensive hotels in Canada. I've taken several strawberry-scented bubble baths in my huge bathroom, and Flash has taken his share of fruity bubble baths, so we both smell fresh as fairies.

We completed our final workout and attended that lame luncheon downtown. They asked Painless to stand up and talk about me, which he did, and then asked me to reciprocate.

"I admire Red Crossley," Painless said. "He is one of the best running backs in the game today and I hope to be able to defend against him on Sunday."

Then I stood up. "Jethro Payne is the finest cornerback around, and I say that with no disrespect to our own players.

"Also, I want to say what a special thing it is for the two Canadian teams to be here, in Canada, playing in the first ever Super Bowl to be held in Canada.

"As for the big game itself, I honestly have no way of knowing who will win, because we're so evenly matched. Probably a turnover or some other unexpected thing will determine the outcome. But I can say with absolutely certainty that we are ready to go."

I felt gratified when all my teammates gave me a brief but heartfelt standing ovation. But then I looked over and saw the stuck-up Stars all giggling and smirking, as if I'd just farted in public.

A few hours later, as we practiced at Northup University, I felt terrific. I had plenty of energy and liked the fact that a bunch of students had stopped by to check us out.

Stuck-up Stars, bring it on!

As I type these words, Francesca and Sheri are in the much-too-big living room of our deluxe suite, entertaining many people, including Lord Larry, Lady Joy, some top people from the Invaders organization and TV people such as Wade Sellers.

I have also been assured that Jeter Davis will be popping in tonight.

Flash and I have definite plans for tonight: Take it easy, relax and hang out in our hotel suite. We will do the same thing tomorrow, too. We want to be well rested for the Super Bowl.

Many well-wishers will be coming and going throughout this evening. Flash and I told Sheri and Francesca to get on the horn to room service and order up plenty for everyone to eat and drink.

But for now, I, Red Crossley, am going to lay here in my paisley bathrobe in my fancy bedroom and write these words on my MacBook Pro computer.

There is a strong possibility that Francesca Roff will serve me a Canadian Comfort over ice now and again this evening.

I want to tell you about last night.

We went to the Northern Broadcasting System's party here in the hotel. NBS supplied the refreshments and L.T. Briggs provided the entertainment. They had the party in the Maple Leaf Café on the second floor of the hotel. The café is a big facility, all glassed in from one end to the other, with spectacular views of the Bayporte rain and heavy traffic. The restaurant also has a terrace that hangs out over the big swimming pool.

Players used to be discouraged from attending these boozy parties because they would get loaded and say or do things to disgrace the NFL. But then Commissioner Roder said that if the players wanted to drink, well, they were grownups, and the prospect of making fools of themselves might make them drink a bit less.

Of course, Commissioner Roder had never partied with L.T. Briggs.

This party was mainly for the Invaders, the local heroes, and not for the stuck-up Stars or their stuck-up fans.

The trouble, so far as I could tell, began when they ran out of Canadian Comfort, so L.T. started drinking whatever they had left. He had them pour rum, vodka, tequila and apricot brandy into a tall glass, and he drank it down.

At some point, Pol Pott walked up to him and said, "L.T., you keep that up and we'll have to take you to Bayporte General to get your stomach pumped."

L.T. said, "I've drunk mouthwash and rubbing alcohol and cooking sherry, and I'm still standin'."

When you caution him about something, L.T. responds by living even more dangerously. A few years back, while romancing one of his girlfriends, L.T. and she were surprised by her angry husband, who shot L.T. twice in the chest. My teammate then got dressed, got into his car and drove himself to the local hospital. The doctors rushed him into surgery and I'm not sure they managed to get him to sleep before operating. He just lay there and healed up over time.

I did observe him one night in Houston as he punched out two police officers on the night before our game against the Texans. We had rented a car and gone to a few nightclubs to listen to country music and pick up Southern women.

On the drive back to our hotel, however, L.T. became disoriented by Houston's sprawl and freaked out a bit. He started driving the wrong way down one-way streets and sideswiping parked vehicles.

Two cruisers finally encountered us and ordered us out of the car. They recognized us immediately and kept their guns holstered. They even offered to escort us back to our hotel and forget the whole ugly business.

Alas, just as we started thanking the officers and getting into our car, L.T. Briggs pointed at the cops and said, "Cops always think they're pretty tough, right? I wanna see how tough you really are!"

Then L.T. Briggs kick some blue asses. Yes, sir, he did.

The Invaders and Texans met in private to figure out how to keep our arrests a secret from the media. We even got to play football the following day. They tell me that our team had to give theirs a high draft pick or something to put things right.

Predictably, then, people felt very uncomfortable when, at the Maple Leaf Café, L.T. Briggs hoisted the actress Claudia Knaack and turned her upside down so that he was holding her by the ankles. He then walked onto the terrace and dangled her over the swimming pool.

L.T. looked bemused rather than amused; that is, he seemed to consider this woman a vexing problem only he could solve. Keep her hanging or let her fall? Which one? And how long is she gonna keep screaming and crying?

People came near yet kept a respectful distance, most of them urging him to haul her back up, the others saying nothing.

Sheri Rawson soon came to L.T.'s side and ended Claudia

Knaack's humiliation. L.T.'s wife, Janice, might have intervened to some degree had she not wandered off with Jack Piros, Eddie Lowelling or someone.

Sheri sidled up to L.T. and said, "She's got a cute pair of legs on her, hey?"

"Yeah, and she's got no panties on! You can see her stuff, too!"

"Now that you have her upside down like this, what happens next?"

"I haven't figured that out yet," he said.

"Maybe just drop her into the pool?" Sheri asked.

"Then she'll get mad at me and try to kick me in the balls."

"Or you could just pull her back up."

"Did she say or do something to offend you, L.T.?"

"Damn right she did. We got to talkin', and she started givin' me the eye, so I said we should go somewhere else and I would eat her out."

"Hmm," said Sheri.

"So then she mouthed somethin' I can't repeat, and I grabbed her. Now I can't figure out what to do with her."

"I empathize with you, L.T.," Sheri said, "but I think you've made it clear to her that she got out of line. Your options now are to let her drop into the pool or pull her back up."

L.T. swallowed hard. "I'm gonna puke any second."

Sheri called down to Claudia, "Can you swim?" and Claudia, her face crimson and arms flailing, screamed out in the affirmative."

"Hands off, L.T.," Sheri

ordered. "I'm gonna barf."

"Hands off," Sheri repeated. "Hear me?"

L.T. unclenched his hands, and Claudia Knaack plunged down into the pool, twenty feet below.

Many guests applauded or laughed. Claudia Knaack hit the bottom of the pool feet first, then darted like a minnow off to the side and climbed out, barely missing the trail of L.T. Briggs' vomitus. Wade Sellers stood waiting for her, a hotel bathrobe draped over his arm.

Francesca Roff tsked. "Now her hair and dress are ruined."

Sheri, Flash and I howled with laughter. Lord Larry and Lady Joy failed to find much humor in that incident, but we assured them that Claudia Knaack, a Tinseltown slut, wanted only to get her name on the Internet gossip blogs and would probably consider her encounter with L.T. a good publicity stunt.

L.T. said he felt great after barfing, and that he wanted some more to eat and drink.

"All of this excitement has made me hungry," said Lord Larry. "Let's go find a big juicy steak."

"I need a Grade A Alberta tenderloin, medium well," said Sheri.

I've just taken a few minutes from writing this book to smoke a joint and contemplate a few things. People think that pot is poison, but they'll drink till they puke. Pot is much less toxic than tobacco.

Sheri was on my mind. Her, Flash and me. Us.

Specifically, I've been thinking about a conversation Flash and I had once in our apartment. We sat in the living room, drinking coffee and listening to Jeter Davis' newest CD. I lay sprawled on the sofa and Flash sat in his favorite leather recliner, and we wondered aloud if we were hungry enough to amble on over to Eli's for cheeseburgers and pick a fight with Eli over the Invaders' chances of becoming a half-decent team.

Sheri had flown down to San Diego to do some modeling, and she'd called us an hour earlier, saying that San Diego hadn't changed

BRIAN ANTONSON

much, it was still full of middle-aged cuties—failed actresses—

running around with faggots, and old rich ladies, newly widowed,

who fed their poodles steak for dinner.

Flash and I have always had half-serious talks about life and the

nature of reality. He, a philosopher at heart, has gone through life

asking, *Why?* while I have always asked, *What's in it for me?*

We talked about Sheri and other things that night. I said, "Flash,

are you aware that Sheri has never really spoken of getting married?"

"I'm aware."

"And your feelings…?"

"Nice for her," he said.

"Really?"

"Yes, it's a good thing that she knows what she wants. Or doesn't

want."

I stretched out on the sofa a bit more, staring at my coffee cup and

wishing it would float away, refill itself and return to me.

"Sometimes," I said, "I wonder where we're all headed."

"Eli's for burgers, right?" Flash said, tapping on his iPad.

"I meant, where we're headed for in this life."

Flash laughed. "Who cares about the big questions when you're getting hungry?"

We both stayed silent for a few moments. Finally I said, "I can't imagine the day when I'll retire. I can't picture myself doing that."

"I'll walk away when the time comes," Flash said, "and I won't regret it for a moment."

"I find that hard to believe," I

said. "Believe it."

"But you like football more than I do, Flash. You will be able to play longer than I will, so it's weird that you would look forward to retiring."

"Do you know how long you and I have been playing

football?" I shrugged. "Most of our lives."

He nodded. "Most of our lives. Doesn't it bug you that we're getting older and that's all we've ever accomplished?"

"Nope."

"Well, that's how I feel about it," he said. "Why did you bring it up?"

"I was just thinking out loud about you and Sheri, if you two were ever going to marry, and if I was going to marry, and if the four of us would retire to someplace in Nevada that's warm and sunny. We could play golf all day."

"I'm never going to move to Nevada, that's for damn sure," he said.

"Yeah, that place sucks."

"I would go to some remote place on another continent," Flash said. "Just go online, find the right place and go. Maybe not even on Planet Earth. Have you heard of that space explorer named Elon Musk? He thinks that in the future, we will be able to live in condos on Mars. Maybe I'll check that out."

"You can't follow the Kodiaks or the Invaders if you're way out on Mars. You would need to know how our teams are doing."

"If I didn't, I would always guess that Lord Larry had the Northup coach fired and that Jack Piros wants to buy better players and get the Invaders into the Super Bowl." Flash paused. "As far as football goes, we've done everything except win the Super Bowl. I mean, if we had played college ball in the States, one of us would probably have won the Heisman Trophy."

"We lost the Provincial Championship for good old Oliver Johnson High," I reminded him.

"Ouch." Then, "You know something? I've been thinking that,

since we're going to the Super Bowl this year, if we win this thing?"

"Become Prime Minister of Canada? You could do it."

"No, I may just take an early retirement and travel and goof off till I have to buy a new suit for Hall of Fame day."

"Bullshit," was all I could say.

"Not at all. If we won the Super Bowl, I would do that."

"That's not exactly what I wanted to hear," I said. "There are many records you can still break."

"Records mean zero. If I don't break them, someone else will, and if I do break them, someone will break mine."

"If you retired, what would you do?" I asked.

"I can tell you what I wouldn't do. I would not get on the football field and run for my life while some big guy tries to tackle and cripple me. I would not force myself to cope with chronic pain. I would not answer the same stupid questions from the same stupid reporters or go to the same luncheons and give speeches. I would just forget about it and think about my present and future."

"I don't know what to say, Flash. I can't relate to any of that."

"That's because you love football and I don't. You'll play for as long as you can, then retire and become the Invaders' head coach.

You'll love it and be great at it. But that's you, not me. I have to figure out what's right for me."

I suppose I thought that if Flash left football altogether, he would put on a suit and manage a company or play around with other people's money. I guessed he would marry Sheri and stay here in Bayporte to keep me company. We could just pretend we were still a threesome at Northup University.

I lay there on the sofa for quite a while, trying to picture life as a Bayporte Invader without Wilbert "Flash" Gortton. It was a hard thing to do and a scary experience.

"What about Sheri?" I asked him. "Where does she fit in? What does she think of your plan?"

"She doesn't know. We haven't talked about it. Anyway, it doesn't matter. Sheri is her own woman. She needs to do what's right for her, and she respects the fact that we need to do our own thing, even if it doesn't necessarily include her."

"Oh, I see. So you retire from the NFL and Elon Musk calls you. 'Flash, your condo is ready,' he says. So you go to Mars. Would Sheri be OK with that?"

"Well, she wouldn't be going with me," Flash said.

"I can't picture you and Sheri apart. I just can't see it, and I don't think you can, either."

"This is how I feel right now, Red. There's always a chance I'll change my mind. As for marrying Sheri, I think marriage is an obsolete institution that destroys loves and lives. Anyway, she and I have been married since we were kids, and that's a very long time."

He added that he had loved her more than anyone or anything in his entire life, but love was a demanding responsibility that had worn him out. Maybe, he thought, it was time for someone else to assume the responsibility of loving Sheri Rawson. He would just as soon go his own way from here on out. He said he wasn't altogether sure I could understand what he was talking about.

I said he was right; I couldn't.

Flash told me that Sheri would join him on Mars if she wanted to go, but she would have to be wholly responsible for herself; he would spend his time looking out for Number One. She would have to feel OK about whatever he did on Mars, be it staring into outer space for hours at a time or trying to lay Martian chicks.

Flash believed that being an NFL superstar had probably prevented him from doing a hundred things he had wanted to try here on Planet Earth. He'd fantasized about being an ice pilot up near Alaska or a bar proprietor in the South Pacific. Or maybe he would go to one of the Japanese islands to stare at the sea and sky and write bad poetry.

"Sounds like fun," I said. "But couldn't you just keep playing for the Invaders and have your adventures during the off-season? Maybe even take Sheri and me along to keep you company?"

"You're missing the point. I have to do things alone. No commitment, obligations or responsibilities. Just me, myself and I. Also, I have to stop being Flash and start being Wilbert." He shrugged. "Just Wilbert, a Canadian guy trying to find himself."

"If I couldn't keep up with the Kodiaks and Invaders," I said, "I would be nothing but miserable."

"Then maybe you should just stay put."

"Look, Flash, I've never met a more gung-ho football player than you. You're the best wide receiver, you get the fans worked up, you give the best interviews after the game. Doesn't that mean anything to you? Could you really walk away from all that?"

"Yes I could. All that effort I put in to get the fans excited, to score those touchdowns, to give good interviews? It's worn me out. I want to learn how it feels to do something different or do nothing at all. But"—he grinned—"I sure would love to win a Super Bowl."

"Me too. But let's go to Eli's now and eat."

"Red, I'll be straight with you. The worst thing in this world for Sheri would be for her to wear a ring, get a license, go to church and get married."

"Doesn't sound so bad to me."

"Oh, but it is. You need to understand that, at her core, Sheri is a chick."

"You've noticed that too, eh?"

"How long have the three of us known each other? Most of our lives, right? Well, have we ever had a fight, dispute, conflict of any kind in all that time?"

"If we did, we forgot about it in fifteen minutes," I said.

"So let's pretend that Sheri and I got married and moved somewhere and she seemed content with our situation. Maybe we were on Mars, and we were happy in our condo. I was happy staring into outer space and contemplating whatever, and Sheri was doing her thing. Do you know what would absolutely, positively happen before too long?"

I shrugged. "Tell me."

"I would do something wrong." He paused. "I would go to the store and forget her cigarettes and Tampax, or maybe I would leave the toilet seat up. Or maybe I would fail to make her come in bed one night. Well, because we would be legally married, that would make her the *boss*, so she would say something about my infraction."

"Might happen."

"So, all of a sudden she's the boss and she's bitching at me over the cigarettes and Tampax or the toilet seat, and our love gets ruined. She's so longer my sweet beloved Sheri, she's this shrew who's ragging on me, and I couldn't cope with that."

I nodded and let his words swirl about in my head for a bit. Jeter Davis' music, wafting from hidden speakers, competed for my attention, but I think Flash's words won out.

"Maybe you're underestimating Sheri," I said.

"I've known her all my life. I'm sure she would turn into a real bitch over time."

"Sure of that? Even Sheri Rawson?"

"Absolutely. It's a sad fact. It's because of her gender. It's as inevitable as saggy boobs and menopause. I just don't want to stick around long enough to see it happen."

"Flash," I asked, "what makes you so damn sure of all this?"

"Years of life experience."

I laughed long and hard. Then I said, "What about men? Are they as bad as women?"

"Men are easier to deal with. If they start to piss and moan, you can just tell them to kiss your ass. They won't be offended, and even if they are, tough titties."

"But women are different," I said.

"Yes. You have to take out the kid gloves and handle women with extreme care. If you forget the cigarettes and Tampax, they think it's because you've stopped caring about them. You forgot the cigarettes and Tampax because you were stoned or you just had other things on your mind."

"But maybe the cigarettes and Tampax meant a lot to her. Maybe she was going into nicotine withdrawal or she was on her period and didn't want to bleed all over you."

"No. If she sent you to the store for cigarettes, she still had half a pack left. If she sent you for Tampax, she was down to her last few, but she still had some left."

"Maybe so," I said.

"It's too bad, but that's just how it

is." "I suppose."

"Red, you asked about where we're all going, and that thought disturbs me because I think we're going nowhere at all."

"I'm having fun."

"But Sheri would trash it all one day just because she didn't get her cigarettes or Tampax. I have known her and loved her all my life, and I know she's the greatest girl ever and you're the best friend I could ever have. I'm aware of that and I'm grateful for it. I have also played football as well as it could be played, but now it's time for something completely different. It bugs me that all I've done so far is play football, party and screw women."

"It means nothing to you that you're rich, famous, successful and surrounded by people who admire you?"

"Lots of people have all that. Everyone can have that kind of life. It's all up for grabs."

"Is that so?" I asked. "So, you've been happy for too long. You need to find some despair."

"I'm not looking for despair. I have always avoided hunger,

poverty and disease whenever I've encountered them. I just need some new scenery to look at and some new music to listen to."

"Sounds like you're in a lonely place right now," I said.

"I don't want loneliness, either. People choose to be lonely. Me, I want some female company no matter where I go. Won't be the same female necessarily, but it'll be someone."

"Doesn't love matter to you?"

"Of course it does. I have loved and been loved, and those have been the greatest experiences of my life. But now I need something new that doesn't involve the people or places I have always known. Shit, Red, I don't even know what I don't know."

"If you want to know more, why not just go back to Northup and get a few dozen Ph.D.s?"

"I'm not after that kind of knowledge. I guess you don't follow me because you really need to be here, where you can follow the Kodiaks and Invaders, and I envy you."

"Well, Flash, I envy you because regardless of all the women I've screwed, I've never had a woman half as fine as Sheri love me. If I had a Sheri, I would be the happiest man in the world. I would never give a thought to going anywhere or doing anything without her. *I'm* the one who should be restless and unfulfilled."

"Don't give up trying, Red. I'm sure things will fall into place for you. Just when you least expect it, you will meet the one for you, and maybe she will sashay into a Bayporte bar. You'll just *know*."

"I wonder how much she'll cost."

"Plenty." We both laughed, and Flash admitted that perhaps he was wrong about these things, or just plain crazy, but he could probably talk better and make more sense if he had a couple of Eli's burgers in his stomach.

"You don't want to move to Mars," I told him. "They don't speak English up there. You'd be on the phone to Elon Musk, demanding your money back."

"Yeah, to hell with Mars. Let's to Eli's and eat some burgers and talk about the Kodiaks and Invaders. Something we know about."

"Just promise me something," I said.

"What is it?"

"Don't retire until we've found a decent replacement for you."

I am still sitting here, writing words with my laptop computer, but now I'm all sweaty and in need of a shower. Things have happened in the past half hour.

I sat up in bed, writing away, with a joint in the ashtray and a Canadian Comfort over ice at my side, when the door opened just a tiny bit and I heard a very familiar and welcome voice.

"Red!"

"Jeter!"

Jeter Davis had arrived. He opened the door, slipped inside, and closed it behind him.

"They told me you were in here. Playing on the computer, hey? Can't you think of anything better to do?" he asked.

"Well, it's a big project I'm working on," I said.

"Lots of fun, Red," Jeter said, smiling. He wore a denim jacket, jeans and a big leather hat. "Lots of fun times in the past, more to come in the future."

Jeter didn't go to parties. He was a walking party. He went through life creating good times.

"You look good, Red. You smell like an interior decorator. You and Flash have been taking those fancy baths, eh? He's out there, too, all dressed up like a pimp. Sheri's looking hot, too, as she always does. Is she still riding Flash's dick?"

"I'm afraid so."

"What a shame. At least you have Francesca out there to keep you warm at night."

"At least I have her," I said.

"Now listen, Red," Jeter said. "You know I never come by empty-handed, hey? Well, I've got your gift in the living room. Wanna see?"

"Do I have a choice?" I asked.

He smirked. "Not really." He disappeared for a moment, and when he came back he had my gift, all five feet seven of her.

"Red," he said, "say hi to Stevie. She's local talent I met recently."

"Hi, Stevie," I said.

Stevie had her blonde hair all piled up, her face professionally made up, her breasts pushed up together. Her eyes wandered, and her mind probably did, too.

"Anyway," said Jeter, "I'll leave you two alone so you can get to know each other just a tiny bit better. Don't worry about your guests. They're about to get an intimate personal performance from Jeter Davis that they'll talk about for the rest of their lives." He winked at me. "Fun, fun, fun, Red. Nothing but fun and good times ahead, eh?"

That was just under an hour ago. Stevie has done her duty, gotten dressed and gone into the living room to enjoy some refreshments and compare notes with Francesca Roff. There I sat, all prettied up and smelling fine, until Jeter Davis came by with Stevie, and now I'm sweaty, smelly and sticky. With Jeter, I simply never know what to expect.

Well, I better stop writing for a few minutes and get all cleaned up.

I'm not sure how other authors write, but I need some privacy and quiet when I'm at the keyboard.

It is now closing in on one in the morning, which means it's now Saturday, the day before Super Bowl Sunday. Our guests departed just after midnight, and I appreciated that. Francesca Roff is spread eagled and sound asleep right next to me. Once she conks out, she goes brain-dead for the next eight hours.

Flash and I wanted an early night, and that's what we got. We spent plenty of time just sitting in the living room and talking about how we were going to steamroller the stuck-up Stars.

Jeter Davis had his guitar, and he played every song he could think of. I enjoyed every moment, and felt as if I had been treated to a personal concert by Bruce Springsteen, or maybe John Mellencamp.

Lord Larry and Lady Joy don't really know Jeter or his music, so they kept asking for songs they did know, but Jeter explained that all he knew was his own music. So Lord Larry and Lady Joy just sat there nice and quiet but not really interested.

Too bad for them.

On Thursday, we had dinner with Lord Larry and Lady Joy, and it went well enough. But dinner with them is always a potentially awkward event, since Lord Larry will inevitably get onto the subject of "minerals and mining" and follow that with what's wrong in professional sports, particularly the NFL.

Lord Larry will also get frustrated with at least one or two servers who got his order right, and he will berate them until half the restaurant is looking at us and muttering to each other. Afterwards, Lord Larry will grumble about the decline of Canadian customer service.

As I say, it went well. We went to a popular downtown restaurant called Wranglers Beefhouse.

Lord Larry minded his manners, although he did slip up a few times about Jews in Hollywood, and he spoke his piece in a voice robust enough to be heard throughout the dining room.

"It's a bloody shame that you young people missed Hollywood when it made movies that were worth seeing," he said.

During a dinner in Los Angeles, he said, "One time I lent a bunch of money to some Hollywood Jew movie producers and never thought I would see my cash again."

Lady Joy didn't mind his remarks. She always just looked around, to make sure she had on the most stylish clothing of any woman there.

Lord Larry did have an issue with the menu the other evening at Wranglers Beefhouse and our server, who was dressed up as a cowboy.

"Howdy, partners, I'm Wrangler Randy and I'm here on the range to serve you," he said.

Lord Larry looked in Wrangler Randy's direction and said, "Young fellow, I don't where you're from, but I think your Western twang needs a bit of work."

Then Lord Larry winked at all of us and glanced at us to see if we got his joke.

Our server said, "The menu is a bit limited. We have specials that may interest you a lot more."

Wrangler Randy adjusted his Stetson hat and hitched up his belt.

Francesca Roff asked about those specials.

"Oh! Well, I have delightful hot and cold soups and salads, plus mushroom and spinach pie. The cold asparagus soup with bits of turkey in it? It is particularly delicious—"

Lord Larry looked up at Wrangler Randy and said, "We want to *eat*, not slurp and graze."

I smiled. Chalk one up for Lord Larry.

Wrangler Rudy said, "Uh, as you can see on the menu, we have a crab cocktail, a salad with Italian and a New York steak." As he spoke, he reached down to where his holster and six-shooter should have been and pulled a Blackberry, or something very similar, out of its leather carrying case. He began pushing its buttons.

"Maybe a scoop of sherbet for dessert, too?" he asked.

"Wait a second," Lord Larry said. "Don't start pushing buttons because we haven't ordered anything yet. We don't want your bloody specials. We *do* want six good steaks and more White Russians. Bring us six Grade A Alberta tenderloins with asparagus and corn on the side. Cook the steaks medium well. Think you can handle that, partner?"

"I hear ya." Wrangler Rudy punched in what Lord Larry wanted and moseyed off, his boots clacking on the floor.

The food tasted good. Lord Larry and Lady Joy asked Francesca Roff about her family, who owned half of Milan or Rome, maybe both. Lord Larry felt that he had done business and made money with some of Francesca's people. Then Lady Joy asked if Sheri had installed the hardwood flooring she had recommended. Sheri said not yet. Lady Joy disliked our apartment and wanted to change things around a bit. Probably, she wanted to evict Flash and me, or at least have Flash marry Sheri and then evict me.

Lord Larry talked about what was wrong with the Canadian economy. Then he commented on Northup's football season. They had won as many games as they lost. He believed that next season would be very much like this one because they simply had too many blacks on offense and too many Wrangler Rudys on defense.

As always, Lord Larry wanted to make a toast once dinner was over and Wrangler Sammy had brought over a fresh batch of White Russians. His toast, as far as I could tell, was to us.

"I love a superstar," he said, "and I still can't believe that I have five of them right here with me."

Lord Larry then went on about how he had helped make us into the superstars we clearly were. Francesca Roff's people, he added, had done the same for her.

"Francesca's father and I have a great deal in common,: he said. "We share a respect for money. I respect the Canadian dollar. What is good for Canada is good for the rest of the world. If people start forgetting that, we're in big trouble."

Lord Larry spoke with affection of Flash, Sheri and me. Lady Joy said a thing or two. Francesca Roff looked bored shitless.

"I'm delighted to have such a beautiful daughter who has all my best qualities and her mother's. I don't understand her values and choices sometimes, but I guess parents never really understand their children.

"Of course," he said, "there have been a few issues. I wish Sheri had gone to a prestigious American school instead of Northup. I think, frankly, that Northup is for local kids who can't get into a better school."

"Smith College in Massachusetts would have been better for Sheri," said Lady Joy.

Sheri just rolled her eyes.

Lord Larry said he still couldn't believe that campus security had caught Sheri in the jocks' dormitory at Northup.

"That was something Rawsons just don't do," he said. Flash, Sheri and I burst into laughter.

"So *humiliating*..." said Lady Joy.

Flash said, "It all turned out OK. Just kids having their fun."

"Lord Larry to the rescue, as usual," Lord Larry muttered.

"Don't overreact, Dad," said Sheri. "Laugh about it. The media didn't find out. No one lost face. It was all funny."

"Is that so?" asked Lord Larry, glowering.

"That was also the night we trashed Clinton Cooke's yacht," Flash said.

"Todd Spofford trashed the yacht," Sheri said.

"Yeah, but we told him to do it," Flash said.

Lord Larry frowned. "Are you saying that someone's yacht was destroyed that night?"

Flash nodded. "Clinton Cooke was a moron from a rich family. He liked to hang out with the jocks. The Cookes owned half a dozen yachts. They didn't miss the one that sank."

"I have yachts myself," said Lord Larry, "but I'd sure get mad if anyone tried to destroy any of them."

Sheri laughed. "It's no big deal, Dad. If you had met Clinton Cooke, you would have been glad to see the yacht sink. In fact, you would been disappointed that he wasn't there to sink with it."

"A yacht is a valuable piece of property that should be respected, no matter how you feel about its owner," Lord Larry said.

Flash said, "I'm not sure why we thought it would be all right to bring those girls back to the dorm. Maybe we thought we were above the law."

I asked, "Wasn't that the same night Todd Spofford kicked the daylights out of a Coke machine?"

Sheri said, "Yes. He vandalized the machine so badly that he could just reach in and drink all the cans of pop inside it. He even dug all of the change out of it."

Flash said, "Do you know why he was so mad?"

Sheri and I laughed some more. We knew.

Todd Spofford was angry because his girlfriend had caught him beating off underneath the dock.

"I find it hard to believe that any half-decent"—he meant Caucasian—"person could bring himself to destroy valuable private property."

"He was mad at his girlfriend about something," I said.

"I hope they expelled Todd Spofford for pulling stunts like those," said Lord Larry. "Vandalism and destruction of private property? That's for terrorists and Commies."

"Spofford was a pretty vicious player," said Flash. "He'd try to break your bones."

"He wasn't too nice off the field, either," I added.

"Do you remember that incident with the Dinosaurs?" Flash asked.

I nearly spat up my White Russian, I laughed so hard.

On a Friday evening in Bayporte before a game Northup had against the University of Alberta Dinosaurs, Todd Spofford headed downtown to check out a Dinosaurs pep rally because he wanted to abduct some male cheerleaders, just for fun.

I had never known any other man who would go to a rival

school's pep rally by himself. But Todd, naturally, could go to the worst part of town at the most dangerous hour without fear. He used to confront truck drivers and pick fights with them just to see if he could take them.

So: Todd went to the pep rally and scored four male cheerleaders. He drove them back to his dorm room and made them get naked and shave each other all over, even their naughty bits.

These were just wimpy little Dino sissies whose fathers had sent them to the University of Alberta to make men of them. So they had to do as Todd said, unless they wanted him to beat the shit out of them.

Todd then painted letters on them purple and gold—Northup's colors—and made them stand alongside each other so that the letters on their chests spelled out GOOF.

Finally, Todd made them sing the Northup school song and masturbate for a few minutes before he let them head back to their hotel.

We sat there in Wranglers Beefhouse, reminiscing a bit more about our childhoods and Northup experiences.

Lord Larry said he felt very gratified that Sheri had never come to him for a handout and that neither Flash nor I had ever sent her to him for money.

Lord Larry, like all other rich men, cried poor-mouth often but acknowledged, or bragged, that he had managed to hide a few bucks from the tax man. But he added that he had a certain amount of money stashed away so that if Sheri needed it—or if she needed it to give to Flash or me because we needed it—the money would be available.

Lord Larry told us that if he and we all remained financially comfortable for the rest of our lives, he would will his estate to certain organizations, provided they demonstrated their gratitude by honoring his memory in some significant way.

He wanted Northup to take a big chunk of his cash and rename their football stadium Lord Larry Rawson Field.

"Who will get your vital organs?" Sheri asked.

"They're going to be buried with me," he said. "Wouldn't I be in a bad way if I came back and had no body to live in? Look, every year they're coming out with different ways and means of prolonging life indefinitely. Do you pay attention to it? Stem cell therapy, nanotechnology, all the rest of it. If something gets cancer, just grow a new body part. We're at six or seven billion people now; how are we going to feed fifteen billion? I say that when people die, it's because God wants them dead."

"Oh, shit," muttered Sheri.

"I'm just saying how it is," said Lord Larry. "Flash plays great football because he has superior physical equipment. If he lost those great big lungs and had to make do with someone's smaller lungs, he wouldn't be half the player he is now. Why do you, Sheri, think you turned out so fine? It's because of your superior genetic makeup.

"When God made people," Lord Larry explained, "He knew there would have to be a special, superior class to make sure everything ran properly. He made some who were superior and others who weren't, and the ones who weren't made a big mess for everyone else. So God got mad about that and intervened again by creating more superior people to clean up that mess and make sure no more messes appeared.

"Everyone once in a while, God would make an earthquake happen, or a *tsunami*, or let some disease go unchecked, just so that a few million inferior people would be wiped out.

"It took some time, but it needed to be done. A few wars helped a lot. The world's population became more manageable, and nobody blamed God for all those deaths. People kept going to church and everything was all right."

Lord Larry took a moment to sip at his White Russian.

"All the while this chaos has been happening, God has chosen some people to be born, become rich and take over the world in a good way. They were corporation presidents, heads of state, military heroes and other powerful decent people such as myself.

"The Rawsons go back a long way. God sent the first of us over to make sure things in the New World got started off properly. He also knew that people like the Rawsons in the New World would see to it that the rest of the world started acting like decent people, too.

"The Rawsons distinguished themselves in all aspects of society. We led thousands of men in both World Wars. I didn't go to war, of course, because God needed me here, where it was safe, to earn huge money, put people to work and be a community leader. But if I had gone to war, I'm sure I would have excelled on the battlefield because I'm a Rawson.

"So," Lord Larry said, "the main wonderful thing that God did for me was to keep here in Bayporte so that I could meet Lady Joy,

141

fall in love and have Sheri. We met at Northup, you know, and while I've always been grateful to my alma mater for all it's given me, I've never felt it was quite good enough for Sheri. But she went there anyway.

"Look at her. That gorgeous hair, those huge eyes, that stunning mind and all the rest of her"—I'm sure he didn't want to brag about his daughter's perfect breasts and heart-shaped ass, at least not in public—"and that took a lot of Rawsons to make."

"Plus some world wars and *tsunamis*," Sheri added.

My MacBook Pro's clock says, "Red, it's time for you to get some beauty sleep." So I think I'll do just that.

I'm beginning to feel anxious and restless. I always do just before a big game, and of course this is the biggest game of my life, though I've had already played in plenty of big ones.

When I awake, it will be Saturday morning, the day before Super Bowl Sunday. That means I'll have another twenty-four hours to fidget and figure out ways of killing time until game day, when Flash and the rest of us will suit up and go to Great Elizabeth Place to kick the crap out of the stuck-up Stars while the world watches.

Between now and then, I'm going to hang around in this deluxe suite and eat fruit, meat and vegetables, and maybe Francesca Roff.

Of course, I will probably have a couple of Canadian Comforts over ice, too. A man has to have some pleasures.

Jeter Davis, of course, is going ahead with his big party in the house he's rented for the Super Bowl. The house is in West Shore, the neighborhood where Bayporte's moneyed elite resides. Some of those people got their money more or less ethically and honestly, while others ripped off other rich people.

I'm sure we'll attend Jeter's party but only for a short while. He's said that he'll have steaks available for those of us who don't want to pig out on short ribs and every kind of salad.

"Red," Jeter told me, "I've ordered in enough scotch, vodka, gin, rum, wine and beer to open my own bar. If any of my guests wants a drink I can't provide, which, to me, is incomprehensible, they could smoke some of my marijuana or hashish instead. I've got plenty of that, too, and it's uncut.

"Also, I have a great idea for live entertainment. I've invited some famous friends—Bryan Adams, Alanis Morissette, Celine Dion,

143

Nickelback, the Tragically Hip—and maybe I can talk them into performing a number or two! See, we're going to have dancing on the lawn, and wouldn't it be a mind-blower to dance as Bryan Adams sang in person!"

"Jeter," I said, "I hate to break some bad news to you, but you can't have dancing outside during your party. This is January in Bayporte, and it's going to rain hard on Saturday night. If Bryan or Alanis or Celine performed outside in the rain, they'd get electrocuted. Better have your dancing indoors."

"I guess you're right. Did I tell you I have some young ladies coming by for the party? Some lovelies who want to embark on modeling or acting careers and are eager to meet single men, or even men with women. These ladies won't be offended if the men or their wives have something kinky in mind."

Flash and I told Jeter that he was sure being generous to his hundred-odd guests. We wondered how much it would cost him.

"Doesn't matter. I tour all the time. I sell a song on iTunes every two seconds. I have more money coming in than I can count, and I think my earnings are going to be pretty stable over the next decade or so. Why not blow a few thousand on your friends?"

For a few minutes tonight, or actually last night, Sheri and I spoke openly and honestly about this book I'm writing. We also spoke about ourselves and each other.

She said she'd read nearly every word and thought it more good than bad.

However, she had some concerns about my characterization of her.

"You make me sound like a store-bought little princess," she said. "I should email Snoop and tell him to edit that stuff about me. Make me deeper, darker and more flawed."

"Also tell him, for me, that if he changes a word of what I've written, he'll find it very different to write with both hands thrust up his rectum," I said.

Sheri wrapped her arms around me and kissed my cheek. I held her and she held me, and I didn't want this physical and emotional intimacy to end, ever. Sheri was the best sister and gal pal I had never had. We stayed quiet for quite a little while, just enjoying each other and being close.

145

Finally, she said, "I've sometimes wondered about my life. The only two people I've ever cared about were you and Flash. I've wondered about what I've missed."

"Absolutely nothing," I told her.

"I've never even had much use for anyone else. Nobody has ever laughed or been happy like you two."

"Lucky you," I said. "Lucky us."

"I want an honest answer now," she said, looking up at me. "A totally honest answer to a very serious question."

"Ask."

"Well, in the Super Bowl, are we going to win or will the stuck-up Stars become the NFL champs?"

"Honest answer?" I asked.

"Completely honest."

"Well, they have quality players and so do we," I told her. "What kind of answer is that?"

"An honest one."

She nodded and patted my chest. "We'll win. You're just jerking me around."

I smiled. "Could be that, too."

146

Sheri then went off into the living room of our deluxe suite to save whatever conversation Lord Larry and Lady Joy were currently monopolizing.

I'm exhausted. Need to sleep. Catch you later.

PART
THREE

SHOWTIME

MAYBE I'LL HAVE to smack the crap out of Francesca Roff before I get around to destroying the stuck-up Stars.

Here is what she did: she ran her mouth about my book to Wade Sellers about my book, which was supposed to be a secret. Then Wade, being the loudmouth fairy he is, announced my book to the world via his blog, which a few zillion people read each day.

I'm not going to dignify Wade by repeating his words here, but if I had wanted the whole fucking world to know about it, I would have told them myself. I think Wade even quoted Painless as saying, "I didn't know that Red Crossley could play football and write a book at the same time."

Francesca Roff has already moaned and wept for forgiveness over this transgression and even comforted me with fellatio, but it was too little too late.

I told Francesca that Wade Sellers better stay out of my road or I'll make bloody sure he's the sorriest motherfucker in the history of Canada.

I'm still totally enraged. I found out about the blog as soon as I woke up and checked my iPad. Normally I keep my temper under control moderately well except when it comes to football, but right now I am livid.

Flash says I'm overreacting. "Many other sports stars have written books. Yours is just the latest. You remember when Canseco wrote that book about injecting steroids up his ass? It's all been said by now, Red. Don't sweat it."

Sheri said, "So now everyone knows you're writing a book about your life in football. Big fucking deal. It's not like you were posing for *Playgirl*, with your stuff hanging out."

"I'm going to have to face my teammates and they'll all know about it. They're going to razz me," I said.

Whenever I'm feeling low, and I listen to music, and whenever I listen to music, I listen to Jeter Davis. I'm sure that his stardom has something to do with it. It's like listening to Bryan Adams, who was born and raised in Canada. You were his pal when he was just a pockmarked, skinny blond kid and you were no better, and you watched him become a star while the two of you were scarcely out of your teens. So Adams becomes more and more famous, while the other rock musicians start fading away, and all the while you're saying to everyone who will listen, "Hey! I knew him when we were kids!"

The main difference, I suppose, is that if I bragged about Jeter Davis that way, I could console myself by shouting out, "Hey! *I'm* famous, too!"

So here I sit, famous Red Crossley, in the early evening of Saturday, the eve of the Super Bowl. Our squad meeting ended a few hours ago and ordered up lunch from room service.

Some Invaders fans, rich out-of-towners who've flown in for the weekend, are having a party down by the pool. Sheri and Francesca Roff are there. Flash and Vernon Braithwaite are answering questions and posing for pictures in one of the main-floor banquet rooms—the Orca Room, I believe—a section of which the sports media have made their headquarters.

Soon, Flash, Sheri, Francesca and I will take a taxi out to Jeter Davis' rented mansion for his party.

Fortunately, at the squad meeting, everyone seemed too preoccupied with other things, like winning the Super Bowl. Eddie Lowelling talked at length about drills, the pregame and halftime shows and other things that interested me very, very little. Eddie said something about how the pregame or halftime show was supposed to have a theme honoring Canada, and I wasn't altogether sure how the

153

vast American viewing public would respond to that.

"We've done all our workouts," Eddie said. "The next time we get on that field, it will be the real deal. So you guys need to get prepared mentally to out there and kick some Toronto ass."

I got a call on my iPhone from my Uncle Joey. I had been expecting to hear from him.

He called to say thanks for the Super Bowl ticket. Regrettably, he had to sell—scalp—the ticket because someone made him an offer he couldn't refuse.

I told him that was OK. I hoped he got a good price for that ticket.

Uncle Joey said he would be watching the game on TV. He had plenty of money bet on the Invaders; did I feel we could make him a rich man today? Did I have a good feeling about things?

I've never felt better about anything in my life, I told him.

And what about Flash? Is he ready to dazzle 'em today at Great Elizabeth Place?

Bet your ass he is, I said.

And Sheri? Is she still the most beautiful girl in town? he asked.

Absolutely, positively. Getting prettier every day.

"Well, Red, you make us proud on that football field tomorrow, eh? Remember that the race isn't always won by the swiftest and the fight isn't always won by the strongest, but that's the way to bet."

"I'll remember," I said.

"Touchdowns, Red," Uncle Joey said.

"Six points," I said.

"Plus an extra point," he said.

"That makes seven," I said.

"Win that Super Bowl, Red," he said.

"It's a done deal," I said. "We're the champs."

Click.

What I wanted to do as soon as I finished up on the phone with Uncle Joey was get ready for Jeter Davis's party. But I couldn't do that because I had some visitors drop by.

Art Jones, the head of the ad agency that employed Sheri, came into our deluxe suite, all smiles and big white teeth.

"Is this a bad time?" he asked. "I can come back later."

One thing about Art Jones: Nobody ever tells him, "Art, this is a bad time. You need to come back later."

I told him, "Art, come on in. We've always got time for you."

He came in and said, "Red, I just wanted to come by and introduce you to a really terrific guy."

I told him I was the only one there. Sheri had gone down to the poolside party, and Flash was talking to reporters downstairs in one of the banquet rooms.

"I know, I know." Art nodded vigorously. "I saw what was happening downstairs before I came up. Hell of a party going on poolside, and I'll bet those sportswriters are asking Flash and Braithwaite every question except how often they jerk off."

"Well," I said, shrugging, "there's not much going on up here except for me, myself and I. I'm just hanging out here till later, when I have a party to go to."

Art Jones came in, followed by a tall guy with a fake tan who carried himself like a model dressed in a Brioni suit and blindly bright shoes. He had a silk pocket hanky and a pink-patterned tie and nothing like a downtown Toronto mover-and-shaker.

Within moments I figured out who Art's friend was: the drunken goof from the party earlier that week who kept calling Flash "superstar" and saying, "You're a handsome bastard."

"Red," said Art Jones, "say hello to a terrific guy. His name is Murphy O'Grady, and he's the president of Royal Tobacco in Toronto.

I said hi.

"Murphy here is our best client," Art told me. "His products are enormously popular throughout Great Elizabeth and everywhere else, and we like to think we helped boost his sales."

Nice to meet ya, I said.

Murphy O'Grady had a soft, low voice, like a female phone-sex worker. "We met a few nights ago at that party. I was so drunk that I don't remember much. Where's your friend?"

"Flash is downstairs with reporters," I said.

Art Jones repeated that Murphy O'Grady was a terrific fellow, even if he *was* a rabid supporter of all Toronto teams.

"I like football in general," Murphy said. "I come out here all the time on business during the NFL season, and it used to be quite easy to get Invaders tickets when the team sucked. But now the Invaders

TOUGH MUTHAS!

are good, and so are the Stars, so it's often difficult as all hell to get tickets."

"But you've got 'em now," said Art Jones, grabbing Murphy's arm. "For the Super Bowl!"

"Crossley," Murphy said, "I saw your two girlfriends down by the pool. I probably offended them a bit the other night at that magazine party or whatever, so I apologized before I came up here. They're a couple of fabulous ladies, you know."

"I know."

"You've got just about all the Invaders down there, Red," Art said. "Got some celebrities down there, too, like Wade Sellers. Too bad you don't have Gretzky or Messier or Steve Nash, too, or some Canadian music stars."

"Maybe next year we'll get the big names." I made sure I didn't tell them about my going to Jeter Davis's party. They probably would have wanted to come along.

"So," Art Jones asked, "are you guys going to win that Super Bowl tomorrow?"

I shrugged. "It'll be difficult, but we're going to do our best."

Art Jones said, "One more thing, Red. Murphy has two great sons

158

at home, Bruce and Russell, in their early teens. And you know what they would love to have? I'll tell you: a cell phone picture of their dad with Red Crossley of the Invaders. They would be so thrilled that they would have it blown up and put it up over their picture of Brad Pitt.

"Yeah, sure," I said. "Let me put my shirt on first."

"Not necessary," replied Murphy. "They'll like it better if you're shirtless."

I shrugged and said OK. I enjoyed posing for that picture with Murphy about as much as I liked a finger wave, but I smiled like a good sport and two flashes later, he had what he wanted and got away from me.

"Fantastic," said Art Jones. "Unreal."

I couldn't help but ask Murphy, "You know that party you mentioned where you got obnoxious with Flash? There was his girlfriend at his side, the one you apologized to downstairs. Any idea of who she is?"

"Should I know her?" he asked.

"Maybe. She's the Royal Girl in all of your billboard and magazine ads from here to Newfoundland. She's everywhere. Her name is

Sheri Rawson."

"That right, eh?" He frowned a bit. "I guess I'll have to take a better look at her next time."

"Beautiful girl," said Art. "The perfect choice for the Royal Girl. The campaign has been terrific."

I told them that Sheri had worked hard on that campaign and had had a great deal of success with other campaigns. They were damn lucky to have her.

"Sure we are, Red," said Art. "You're absolutely right. Anyway, Red, we have to go now. Have a good Super Bowl tomorrow."

I said I would certainly try.

I can hear the door open, so it must be Flash, Sheri and Francesca. They're all headed for Jeter Davis's party, so I guess I am, too. Tomorrow I will join the team for breakfast and we'll get all taped up for the big game. We won't be at Jeter's for long, since I need to get rested up.

Since I have the biggest day of my life happening tomorrow, I don't know if I'll get much sleep between now and then.

THE SOUND SYSTEM here in our deluxe suite is turned down so as not to disturb anyone by the poignant voice of Jeter Davis or my off-key humming and moaning. His music soothes me, and if it doesn't, I'm beyond soothing. I sit here in the early morning of Super Bowl Sunday, staring at those items we value on New Year's Day: Tylenol 3, orange juice, coffee.

I have used each of these and they have helped so far, but not enough. What I really need is time, but that's simply not available.

I should be dead right now, because last night I drank enough Canadian Comfort to kill three Red Crossleys. Someone should have stopped me, because everyone knew I was getting pissed on Super Bowl eve.

When this book is published in several months, everybody who reads it will be amazed at what happened on the night before the big game.

As parties go, Jeter Davis's was almost as powerful as Hurricane Katrina, and I would have been disappointed had it been anything less than that.

When our taxi pulled up, I felt grateful that we didn't need to find a parking space because the streets were lined with vehicles. The sky, a mottled dark gray, seemed about to pour rain on us, and Jeter had the common sense to keep his festivities indoors. I couldn't tell, as we bounded up the driveway and reached the front door, if he had any windows open, but the thump of rock music blared out into the yard.

Jeter had rented one of those stone mansions in West Shore, near Lord Larry and Lady Joy's house and country club and not terribly far from Northup University. The mansion, owned by Hong Kong zillionaires who didn't reside in it and seldom visited it, had become a favorite of Hollywood film crews because of its grand size and fine acoustics. Plus, the front and back yards were big and tall, broad trees surrounding the entire property made it practically invisible from the street.

Once we stepped inside the house, we saw a hundred or more people we had never met. By Bayporte's standards, this gathering qualified as a costume party.

Most of the men looked like Wrangler Randy or Moses, and the women were dressed like Native squaws or beach girls or cowgirls or street prostitutes. I saw many skin-tight leather shorts, tight skirts, push-up bras, mesh tops and jaded faces.

Conspicuous throughout were Canadian Airways flight attendants, wannabe actresses and models and their girlfriends, all parading about like Jeter's little helpers.

We couldn't help noticing them because they were all nude but for oversized, flimsy white T-shirts emblazoned with the words BAYPORTE INVADERS SUPER BOWL CHAMPIONS in our team's colors. Their breasts, bushes and backsides were clearly visible through the cheap material. We looked from one woman to the next, then back again, to see who had better equipment.

Food and beverages, abundant and fragrant, filled the vast living room. Barbecued ribs sat steaming on a huge table along with fixings such as onion rings, French fries and salads.

The entire living room looked like a church, with its ultra-high ceiling and oversized paintings of smug, unsmiling—and certainly toothless—men who were religious leaders or other highly placed holy people.

A bowtied man stood behind each of the bars, of which there seemed to be half a dozen, even in the bedrooms. I kept walking through the house and ended up in what I supposed was the master bedroom, about as big as Oliver Johnson Secondary School's gymnasium. Inside I beheld two king-sized beds pushed together to form one huge sleeping place.

As we wandered through this house, some of Jeter's T-shirted, braless, unpantied girls approached us for conversation. One in particular, scarcely old enough to drink, had medium-length dark hair and sparkling blue eyes and acted as if she'd already had a few hits from the long, thick joint in her right hand. She explained that Jeter had hidden those joints throughout the house. "But they're easy to find, and if you can't find one, just ask me and I'll show you."

She said her name was Alexis and that he lived off her parents' money. She skied in Whistler, surfed in Australia. "I like to dance at Combat Zone." She added that she worked as a flight attendant for Canadian Airways. "I do it for pocket money and the flight perks. What really turns me on is getting high, partying all night and boffing handsome men."

Another girl joined us. She had yellow-blonde hair that ended just above the crack of her ass. She wore big glasses and spent most of our conversation gnawing on a rib.

She told us her name was Hannah and she had spent a year studying at the University of Toronto, the following year at the University of Alberta and next year at Northup. She wanted to go to Europe to study but said that over there they were just trying to be like us. She had also spent a year in central California, illegally picking vegetables.

Hannah said that her guru understood far more than Jesus or even Hitler, and that Hitler understood far more understood far more than most people did, which made him very dangerous and despised.

Her most treasured experience happened in Hawaii, when she fell asleep on the beach and awoke with third-degree sunburns over half of her body. Severely dehydrated, she had visions comparable to those of Tolstoy until the paramedics arrived and delivered her to a hospital to be iced down and loaded up with a sugar-and-salt IV solution till her delirium passed.

Hannah wondered if Sheri or Francesca wanted to go down on her. "I'm very responsive. I'll make sure it's good for both of us."

She was OK-looking, too, for a brainy girl. But when she looked at our women and didn't get the answer she wanted, she just skulked away, a long piece of rib hanging out of her mouth.

The next T-shirted girl, Bonita, taller and more muscular than the others, reminded me of a tennis player or swimmer, with her thick legs and broad shoulders. A premed student at Northup, she despaired of ever graduating and seeing her first patient.

Bonita said she felt bored with this party. "It's just a bunch of people eating, drinking, smoking pot and making pointless talk. There's no direction to it. It's just harmless energy going around in circles."

"Is there something wrong with that?" I asked. "I'm having a nice time."

"Then good for you. But what about the rest of us, like me?" "What about you?" I asked, not at all rhetorically.

"I was among the first people to arrive at this party," she explained. "There are maybe a hundred guys here, right?"

I nodded.

"I've asked about two dozen of them to come upstairs with me, and every one of them said no."

Flash and I, almost at the same time, asked Bonita what she wanted of those guys.

"I wanted them to make me happy," she said. "I wanted them to turn me on."

Flash and I said those guys were fools if they didn't want to turn her on.

Then we looked at Sheri, who was smiling at us. "You don't get it," she said.

"Nobody gets it," Bonita said.

Flash said, "I get it all the time. I get more than I want, sometimes."

Bonita rolled her eyes and told Flash and me that we were really lame. She said that we were just like the others. We had no desire to turn her on and make her happy.

"Don't you know what turns a woman on? Let me clue you in. Have you been upstairs yet? Have you seen the master bedroom and its bathroom?"

We said yes.

"Well," she said, "what *I* want is to get naked and lay down in that nice big bathtub and have some guys come in and do my thing, which is golden showers."

Flash and I looked at each other. Then we looked at her and told her we had never heard of golden showers. What was it?

Bonita heaved a huge, exasperated sigh and said, "Why is everyone so lame? Look, boys, what I want is to lay down in that bathtub and have guys make wee-wee on me. Understand?"

Sheri burst out laughing. "I think they understand now."

Flash and I stared at Bonita, thinking that her luscious bod had been created for things other than being urinated upon.

Flash said, "Bonita, I think we can improve your evening and make it all worthwhile if we can find a teammates of ours named L.T. Briggs."

I had to stop writing for a moment and answer my iPhone when Snoop called. That distinguished Canadian journalist wanted to know how I felt on the morning of the Super Bowl.

"I think the stuck-up Stars wear the same color as the Calgary Dinosaurs," I said.

"I think you're right," Snoop said.

"Then how can I take the stuck-up Stars seriously if they get on the field dressed as the Dinos?"

"Your voice sounds hoarse," he told me. "Are you sure you got a good night's sleep?"

"How's everything going at your end?" I asked. "Busy week for you, eh?"

"I've got my flunkies doing most of the main stuff," Snoop said. "I'm quite interested in the progress of your book, though."

"I'm making all kinds of progress, thanks to my MacBook

Pro." "Care to show me any of it?" he asked.

"You'll see it all when I'm done. Then you can take out your blue pencil and make suggestions."

"Do you have plenty of depth and detail?" he wanted to know. "Have you written a real page-turner?"

"You won't want to put it down," I told him. "I've even made sure that my readers knows whenever I have a drink, it's Canadian Comfort over ice. Once my reader is done with my book, he'll consider me part of his family. Speaking of family, how's your missus?"

"She's been fine lately, Red. We don't fight because I'm rarely at home. But don't ever believe anyone who tells you that marriage is a bad institution. Compared to being a blind homosexual quadriplegic, being a husband is the best deal in town."

"I have to go now, Snoop. I have meds to take, fluids to drink and a nap once the meds and fluids kick in."

"Just remember one thing, Red. That book of yours is going to sell much better if you Invaders win that Super Bowl this afternoon."

"No fuckin' shit," I said.

"Will you have the manuscript ready for me on hard copy sometime next week? Is that the plan?"

"Expect it when you see it," I told him.

"Can't you be a bit more specific?"

"No. I need to cool out and rest. I have places to go and people to see. But I will get to you before too long and we can go over my manuscript. We'll make sure the publisher has it by the summer."

"Also," Snoop asked, "did some good-looking, weird woman fly out there to interview you?"

"Sure did. She was kind of insistent that we get together and talk."

"She bugged me for an interview, too. She seemed very brainy and full of herself."

"Yes, she did," I said. "She said she was the boss of some really hip women's magazine and wanted some kind of in-depth piece on me. I kind of just blew her off. Didn't give her much."

"Did she ask you a bunch of personal questions about your behavior off the football field?"

"Oh, she wanted to know if I got an erection whenever I scored a touchdown or got tackled by a black guy. I'm surprised she didn't ask me if I wanted to screw my mother and kill my father," I said.

"I believe she's really hot stuff in New York literary circles. Maybe she was paying you a big compliment by flying out this way just to interview you."

"She was a ditz," I said. "We met downstairs in the Maple Leaf Café and she ordered iced tea, then she got pissed off because the iced tea was sweet and she likes it unsweetened. Well, this is Canada, and we always drink it sweetened up here. Then she started telling me what a powerful person she was in Manhattan, how she was sort of the boss of her magazine and some other publications. Like I gave a shit."

"Remember her name? Was it Fannie Bueller?" Snoop

asked. "Could have been. Sounds about right."

"Yeah, she's a big deal, all right. She's the editor of a whole bunch of magazines out there. I hope she liked you and won't be doing a hatchet job on you."

"I don't know if she liked me or not. She kept dropping names of her famous friends back East and seemed let down when I didn't know who they were. She told me several times that she knew zero about football, as if that were something to brag about. She seemed to think a football player was some kind of caged beast that needed to be hosed down and thrown a pound of raw meat at the end of the day."

"Did you give her a jump?" he asked.

"Not exactly. I just looked bored, alienated and restless. I think that turned her on, and she went away frustrated that I didn't try to look up her skirt."

Snoop said he had to go fix some of his interns' ungrammatical, unsyntactical news stories, and I said I had to hydrate and medicate. He wished me good luck in the Super Bowl; I told him we needed touchdowns, not luck.

Anyway, at Jeter's party, we discovered our host in the large backyard, sitting under a tree with some of his guests surrounding him. The ground felt dry and the forecast rain hadn't fallen yet.

"Anyway," he said, "what were we talking about?"

"Gourmet food," someone said.

"Underaged females," said someone else.

"Two of my favorite subjects," said Jeter.

Alas, as we sat around Jeter, his friends passed around those long, thick joints, and we smoked them, mainly because we thought they would go well with the ribs. He didn't have any steaks, or if he did, they were already in people's stomachs. I overheard someone say that the T-shirted girls had scarfed them all down or put them aside to take home.

I need to have the youth of Canada and elsewhere to know that I, Red Crossley, always prefer a Canadian Comfort over ice to cannabis, although I truly believe that pot is innocuous enough and won't turn anyone into a drug maniac despite what the Province of Great Elizabeth says.

That evening, I drank and smoked pot. I started with a Canadian Comfort over ice, then decided I should drink very little on the evening before the Super Bowl. However, I *was* at a party and wanted to enjoy the refreshments like everyone else. So I toked up, but that gave me the munchies, and I didn't want to pig out on ribs, so I went back to drinking Canadian Comfort over ice. I got high on booze and pot, and staggered about like a skid row loser. Now, unfortunately, it's the morning of the big game and I'm too hung over to do anything except seek relief.

Yuck.

But I was telling you about the party.

We sat with Jeter and the others for about an hour, until the people got too weird and stuff happened that you won't believe but I'll tell you about anyway.

After time passed in that backyard and most of us got sick of listening to Jeter, some guy with a camera around his neck came up and said he wanted to take a picture. Jeter said fine, because he had hired the guy to take pictures that Jeter would use to decorate his home and maybe even use for the cover of his next CD.

We all kept sitting on the lawn, yakking and laughing, when a girl not wearing one of those cheap T-shirts and not some sort of lacquered-up whore, went over to pose for the photographer.

The girl, a Native squaw in jeans and a suede vest, pulled off her vest with much to-do and crossed her arms over her breasts for the longest time before giving us a good long look at her breasts, as if she were a stripper and we had to wait and beg throw money till she was ready to show us her zoomers. Like hers were better than everyone else's.

I didn't like her attitude. She was a beautiful woman, raven-haired and petite, the kind who would throw things at you during a fight.

But some other guests, once this woman was naked but for her jeans, started applauding and wolf-whistling. She started smiling and doing cheesecake poses for the photographer. She had undressed for him, not us, and, as I say, she acted as she were doing us the world's biggest favor by getting topless for us.

We watched this little show for a few minutes. Then Sheri, who had smoked and drunk more than usual and sat sprawled on the grass, said, "She's not so hot. I could do better if I could get off my ass, but I don't think I can."

Flash and I laughed, which pissed her off.

"I could, too," said Francesca, sitting next to Sheri and just as inebriated.

Jeter Davis said, "Yeah, if you ladies could get up off your drunken bums, you could entertain us all. But you can't, so shut up."

"If I could get up," said Sheri, "I would strip for you."

"Remain seated," I said, "and be very quiet."

Jeter said, "If you could get up, Miz Rawson, what would you do for us? Smile pretty and wink at the camera, the way you do on those billboards and busboards? I believe we've seen that already."

"Oh, I'd put on a hell of a show, Mister Dhaliwal." Sheri giggled.

"Yeah, there wouldn't be a limp dick here," said Francesca.

"Well," said Derek, "I've been all around the world a few times by now and I've seen plenty of things. But what I *would* like to see, that I haven't seen yet, is the pair of titties owned by the heiress to the Rawson mining fortune. Plus her Roman heiress friend Francesca, if she's so inclined."

Jeter added, "Of course, I can't speak for the rest of these people."

Sheri said, "If we weren't so drunk and stoned, we would show you our stuff. But we just can't seem to get up."

"What we need," said Jeter, "is a few gentlemen around here to help these two ladies get up and show us their stuff. Who wants to help?"

Nobody spoke but everybody laughed.

"No takers, eh?" said Jeter. "I guess we all figure that their zoomers are pretty much like everyone else's."

Sheri and Francesca had both lain there like patients sprawled out on stretchers. Both started trying to sit up.

"Well, if these two cuties are too incapacitated even to sit up," said Jeter, "maybe Flash or Red would be willing to tell us about these ladies' zoomers."

"To hell with that," Sheri said, rising to her feet with a Canadian Comfort over ice in her hand. "We need to show these people our stuff, hey, Frannie?"

"Focking-A," replied Francesca.

Sheri wore a black turtleneck and a pair of green corduroy pants that fit her hips snugly without a belt. She wore such an outfit whenever she didn't know what else to wear and didn't know what kind of weather she would be in. Francesca wore tight faded Levi's and a black crewneck sweatshirt that she bought in Milan for four hundred dollars.

Sheri struggled to her feet and did a tiny curtsey. "Ta-da!"

Francesca looked up. "Hey! How you do that?"

"Through physical determination and mental discipline," Sheri replied.

Flash and I looked at each other as if to say, *How far will our women go with this nonsense? Are they really going to strip here, in front of everyone?*

Sheri whistled, loudly enough to be heard by every taxi driver in Toronto, and laughed at all the heads that turned in her direction. Then she whistled again, because she noticed that a few people had mostly ignored her first one.

"Ladies and gentlemen, check it out," Sheri said, looking down at Flash and me to see if we got her joke. 'Ladies and gentlemen, check it out' is Art Jones's favorite line when he takes clients out for the evening to bars where hookers hang out.

Some of Jeter's guests wandered over to join us, mostly people from indoors who came out because they had heard Sheri's whistles.

"Red," Francesca said, "I need to get up. Help

me." "How come?" I asked.

"Because I need to get naked."

"Oh," I said. I helped her up and she swayed a bit as she stood by Sheri's side, the two women standing before all of us as if making a business presentation. I really felt unsure as to how far Sheri would go with this, nor did Sheri seem to know.

"I need everyone to pay attention now," Sheri announced, "because I want to show you something that I'm very proud of."

"Me too," said Francesca.

"What is going to happen," Sheri explained, "is that Miz Rawson—that's me—and Miz Roff—that's her—are going to strip for your onanistic pleasure." She paused and looked bemused. "But first, I need to know where the hell my drink went."

Flash handed Sheri her Canadian Comfort over ice.

"Thank you. That was very kind. I'm going to tell Jethro Payne what a gentleman you are." Sheri took a gulp of liquor and handed it to Francesca, who held it for her.

"Now," Sheri said, "the first thing is for me to get this turtleneck off." She unbuttoned her slacks with some drunken difficulty, unzipped them and pulled up her black garment until it peeled back like an angry, nappy, charred skin.

Right away, she thrust her turtleneck at Flash as if it were a football with which she expected him to sprint across the yard.

"You like?" Sheri asked, displaying her magnificent breasts. Everybody applauded. Flash handed her a fresh Canadian Comfort over ice and a tobacco cigarette. So she just stood there, topless, smoking and drinking, with her world-class zoomers on display for all to see. And she really didn't care if the whole world looked.

I had known Sheri all my life and knew she was just having fun with this gag. Otherwise, I might have considered her behavior provocative, even exhibitionistic, as if she were trying to start an orgy or at least inviting the men at the party to gang-bang her. And that would have freaked me out. Flash, too.

Sheri's zoomers, of course, are wonderful. I've seen that matching set of collector's items a thousand times and been thrilled and delighted by their size, gravity-defying pertness and perkiness. Her nipples, rosy pink and often standing at attention, have winked and blown kisses at me.

She stood there for a couple of minutes, grinning and drinking and smoking. "But wait," she said with the breathless urgency of a late-night TV pitchman hawking kitchen wares, "there's more."

"I would guess," she added, "that if there's one thing most people in this world want when they see a set of marvelous mammaries like mine, it's to see a hot, fresh, creamy *pussy* belonging to the same body."

"Yeah!" shouted Jeter Davis as everyone applauded. "Show us!"

Flashed looked up at Sheri. "You're truly blessed to have what God gave you."

"Amen to that," she replied. "And fortunately, I'm going to show all of you, right now, my God-given blessings."

She began tugging at the waistband of her corduroy slacks. "I've been told that my stuff smells better than the interior of a brand-new Maserati and tastes better than pumpkin pie."

Sheri had to struggle a bit to get her slacks off. At one point she balanced herself precariously on one leg, heehawing and guffawing with a cigarette between her taut, pursed lips.

"Sheri's stuff," Flash explained to the crowd, "is tough. She has tough stuff."

"Fucking right it is," Sheri said. "It's been through a lot."

So there she stood, totally naked in public, being applauded by, whistled and gawked at by a bunch of people fully dressed. She ran an exhausted hand through her strawberry blonde hair, her face covered by a light sheen of sweat.

Jeter, who knew as well as the rest of us that Sheri's stuff—and the rest of her—belonged to exactly one man, leaned over to that man and said, "Flash, tell us the truth: Is she is fine as she looks?"

Flash shook his hand. "She does her best."

Sheri, paying no attention to them, struck one pose after another, and the photographer snapped so many pictures that you would have thought you were at the Oscars.

Soon she grew bored with the attention—the wolf whistles and shouts for her to masturbate to orgasm in front of us—and turned to Francesca, who stared at Sheri's stuff with the deepest fascination.

"Your turn, girlfriend." Sheri turned to Francesca and, after a few pulls and tugs, had the Roman beauty stripped down to her birthday suit, too.

As everyone began making noise again, Jeter got up and wrapped his arms around the naked ladies' waists while the photographer snapped away at the beaming, drunken threesome.

"I want this to be the cover art on my next CD," he said. "Maybe I'll write some songs about the titties and pussies of rich bitches from Canada and Italy and how they keep my right hand busy late at night."

At about this point we reached the beginning of the end of our evening because many other girls started stripping, too. All of Jeter's T-shirted girls pulled off their garments and threw them into the air, and someone turned up the music—Alanis Morissette, Bryan Adams, Nelly Furtado and Nickelback had ignored Jeter's invitations, so he simply played his own songs and CDs of dance hits. Everyone outside could hear it and started to boogie.

Some faggots started dancing with Sheri and Francesca, then the faggots started checking each other out instead of ogling Sheri and Francesca, as anybody with any sense would have done. Go figure.

For the longest time, the sight became surreal: all that naked female flesh grooving on the beautiful vibrations as the thump of dance music blared throughout West Shore.

Unfortunately, the faggots started stripping, too, and everybody got grossed out and turned away at the spectacle of naked queers who were built like twelve-year-old girls wasting away from AIDS.

Jeter, Flash and I simply sat back and watched. We picked out the people we should invite to future parties. One of the flight attendants sauntered by and stopped to visit with us.

"Awesome!" she exclaimed to Jeter as she stood naked, toking away on a joint. "Say, let me ask you something: What's the most memorable thing anyone has said to you in bed?"

Jeter said, scratching his head, "Dirtiest thing I've heard in bed?"

"No, most memorable. Like when you're really getting it on and she said something really off the wall."

"Someone said, 'Fuck me, baby, ooh yeah' not too long ago," Jeter said.

I nodded.

"Oh, that's boring," said the flight attendant. "My all-time favorite is, 'I'm gonna come on your cock.' I heard that in a porn movie years ago." To Jeter she said, "Wanna go inside with me?"

Jeter nodded and the two of them headed into the house. Then I heard a familiar voice and smiled at the sight of L.T. Briggs, but I felt totally blown away that, standing next to him, were Painless and Ralph Stefani, the latter being the quarterback of the stuck-up Stars.

"I was at Eli's, tucking away a few burgers," explained L.T., "when I seen these two losers come in. So I asked them if they wanted to eat something that tasted a lot better than cheeseburgers, and here we are." He looked around and added, "Seems like we come to the right place."

Flash and I got up and shook hands with Painless and Stefani. Both men were dressed in T-shirts, jeans and leather jackets, the kind of apparel celebrities wear when they don't want to attract even more attention than they normally do.

"Real nice party, Red," said Painless, smiling as he smoked a joint.

184

He was already half wasted.

Next to him, Stefani said nothing; he just drank from a bottle of Coke. But soon I learned that his Coke was half bourbon and he was so fucked up he couldn't speak. It didn't matter that much; all we could talk about was Commissioner Roder and how glad we were that he was elsewhere. Roder didn't care much where we were or what we did, as long as the highlights or lowlights of our parties didn't show up on YouTube or someone's blog. Roder feared that if key players from both teams socialized right before a big game, they could agree to fix things, bet big and win pots of money. Or Roder feared that a private meeting of key players, made public through the miracle of the Internet via someone's cell phone, would cause the rest of the world to perceive us as rigging the game.

Nonsense, I tell you.

Anyway, the appearance of Flash, Painless, Stefani and me in a little huddle freaked out Sheri and Francesca, who hurried back into their clothes and stood by us like meek little girlfriends. When I introduced her to Painless and Stefani, Francesca said, "Aren't you the stuck-up Stars?"

Painless and Stefani ignored her remark because they were both too busy checking out the women who were still dancing naked. Soon, Flash and Painless kidded each other about tomorrow's big game.

"You gonna play hard tomorrow, or are you gonna take it easy?" Flash asked.

"I'm gonna play wherever the ball's coming my way," he said. "Onliest time I take it easy is when I'm on the bench."

"I feel fast, my man," Flash said. "Fast and furious."

"Fast don't mean shit if you ain't got the ball." Painless

smiled. They both laughed, briefly and humorlessly.

Sheri said, "Painless, why don't you take one of these girls with the pretty titties upstairs and let her come on your cock?"

We all laughed, especially Painless.

The two Stars left to get laid, and Jeter came by with Hannah the nurse and an NFL football stuffed with fragrant marijuana. For a few minutes we handed it back and forth and made jokes about its stinkiness. Then Jeter said we should divide up into a couple of teams and play some touch football, seeing as how big the yard was. Flash and I would be on one side, Painless and Stefani on the other. Invaders versus Stars, one might say. Sheri and Francesca on our side, and a couple of the naked girls on theirs. A couple of homosexuals on their team, and a couple on ours. Jeter would play on our side, since he was a native Bayporter and a devout Invaders fan.

Truthfully, the game went badly. Flash and I were too stoned to do much, as were Painless and Stefani, who were cranky because they were too fucked up to make it with the girls. The queers, sweaty and crimson-faced, took over the game, passing and receiving the ball and tackling the girls by pulling their hair.

So far as I know, the party is still happening even as I sit here in my deluxe suite waiting for my meds to kick in. We all came back here right after the touch-football game. I flopped into bed and drifted into and out of a restless sleep.

I assume the rest of Jeter's guests made it back home all right, and that Painless and Stefani are in no condition to play football today. I guess that's why Jeter seemed so eager to have those guys at his orgy last night; he wanted to compromise them for the big game today.

But it's time for me to get myself straightened out. I need to meet up with the team for breakfast and then head out to Great Elizabeth Place to kick the ever-lovin' shit out of those worthless, dick-less, scumbag Toronto Stars.

I won't be writing anything for several days, because after the game is over, whether we win or lose (and I really shouldn't give us the option of the latter), I am coming back to this deluxe suite at the Hotel Bayporte and wade in a river of Canadian Comfort for a few days. This, of course, will be our final game of the season, so Flash and I will be taking an extended trip to Decadence City.

Here is what we will do:

Flash will fly out to New York City for several days to appear on some TV shows. He says he has other business there, too, though I'm not sure what that might be or that it's even any of my business. Francesca says she'll fly out there with him and then catch a flight back to Rome so she can check in with her people and show them that is she still alive and well. That life with Red, Flash and Sheri hasn't irretrievably corrupted her yet.

I'm going to hang out here in the hotel while Flash and Francesca do their things back east.

I'm going to stay in this hotel and drink, watch TV and sleep. Maybe I'll get laid, too, but probably not, since I'm not expecting to be in the mood for that right after the Super Bowl. Sheri will be here,

BRIAN ANTONSON

too, doing a couple of modeling gigs but mainly just being here in case I need company, which I probably won't, since I'll have Canadian Comfort over ice for that.

Once Flash and Francesca return, the four of us will go to a faraway place, the same place Flash, Sheri and I have been going for the past several years right after the football season ends.

It's just the four of us—Flash, Sheri, myself and the young lady of my choice—heading off to the Hawaiian Islands for about a month just to eat, sleep, drink and fuck.

For me, there simply is no other way to recover from a brutal NFL season.

Our Hawaiian getaway is in a secluded part of the Big Island. All we do is bring a few changes of clothing, a laptop computer and a good attitude. We use the laptop as our only way of communicating with the rest of the world; we have no phone or TV there, just a valley, mountains, trees and ocean. And peace of mind, of course.

By that time, the Super Bowl will old news, mostly forgotten already unless it was spectacularly exciting, and I will have read about it and looked at the images on *Sports Illustrated* online.

I will also have obsessed over it, regardless of the quality of my

189

performance, and I will have scrutinized Flash's participation but will not say so. Lord Larry, Lady Joy, Sheri and Art Jones, sitting in the stands, will see it all, too, and, over time, will tell me what they thought, whether or not I want to hear from them.

So, I will be in Aloha-land with my MacBook Pro, finishing this book, and my female guest and my two greatest friends to distract me from my writing, and that is where I will be when I give you my version of what happened on Super Bowl Sunday in Canada.

Super Bowl Sunday in Canada, eh? That still sounds weird to me.

Now I need to get busy.

Well, I'm finally back at this book, after doing plenty of procrastinating. I'm here on the Big Island, of course, where there is relatively little to do, and all the time imaginable in which to do it, so what little there is to do often doesn't get done at all. For some reason, maybe my conscience started getting on me, I decided to boot up my MacBook Pro and get back to work on this book.

First off, I need to explain that this been different from the end-of-season getaway I expected and desired.

Flash was one of the issues, and Francesca was the other one.

Both were no-shows.

Sheri and I arrived in Hawaii as we had planned, and we waited all day for them to show up, and when they didn't, we weren't all that worried, because you just never know about people, do you?

So, on the following day, when they still hadn't come, I checked me email and found a message from Francesca Roff, who, informed me that, while in New York, she had met up with Wade Sellers and agreed to go goofing off with him all over Europe because he was going there to star in a movie and he might even get the director to put her in it somewhere. She said sorry about Hawaii, but when opportunities come along, you have to go with them. She asked me to wish her luck.

I emailed her that Wade Sellers was a rubber-wristed, screaming fairy and nobody likes a fag hag, anyway.

She said his sexual orientation was his own business; that I should have known of her screen acting aspirations and tried to help her; that Wade was gentle and kind and knew many highly placed people who could get her screen tests and whatnot, and what had *I*, Red Crossley, ever done for her except shoved his thing into her whenever he felt like it?

I emailed her that she had really pissed me off.

She replied that Wade Sellers told her she was just biding her time with me and she was just my "latest squeeze." After all, Wade said, Red Crossley was just a football player who would end up crippled and running a restaurant one day. Most important, Wade observed, it was obvious to the whole universe and beyond that Red was in love with Sheri even if he couldn't have her because his best friend, Flash, was banging her silly.

I told Francesca she was the best whore any guy had ever had.

Flash Gortton is a different story.

When he didn't arrive here when expected, we merely assumed he had stayed in Manhattan to get stoned and chase women. We left messages on his iPhone and called a few mutual contacts, who had no idea where he was. Just as we were starting to freak out just a tiny bit, one morning we received this email from him:

Red & Sheri,

Hello from Invader "Flash" in Tahiti, Tripoli, Timbuktu or somewhere else. Some parts of world are dangerous, full of civil war and leaders being assassinated. Stay safe and stay put, you two. "Flash" loves his Red & Sheri but loves himself more & is trying to find that self but the little bugger keep getting away. Search to find self may take a lifetime or a bit longer; need to call Elon Musk re: progress of construction on Mars condo. "Flash" thinks Red should start shopping for Sheri's cigs and…other things. Let's all meet up in my condo way out there one day with lots of Canadian Comfort over ice.

Love & peace, "Flash"

If I didn't know better, I would say he was telling us to fuck off. Or that he'd fucked off.

I am convinced that, if Flash is in trouble, we would know about it and Lord Larry could fix it with a few phone calls. Plus, I'm doing a pretty good job of talking myself into believing that Flash will arrive here pretty soon, with plenty to share about his adventures while I sit here writing about the Super Bowl which we would probably rather forget.

Sheri says Flash made his message clear. "I'm afraid he's run away from home."

Around our little rental beach house, Sheri pretends that Flash's absence means little, but I've noticed that she refuses to delete his email from the computer. She also spends entirely too much time out by the water, gazing into the sexy Hawaiian sky, as if she expects to see a helicopter come buzzing in at any moment with her man at the controls.

"Religion is his preoccupation," Sheri said. "He's obsessed with figuring it all out."

"Good luck with that," I said.

We got up from the kitchen table and went out onto the beach. Then we both sat spread-eagled on the sand and closed our eyes with our faces tilted up towards the sun, as if we were speaking before the Creator Himself.

"Did Flash tell you much about when he was a kid and his grandmother force-fed him Christianity?" Sheri asked.

Not much, I said.

"Well, she dragged him off to church, then made him watch the TV evangelists and listen to the ones on the radio," Sheri said.

"Yeah, he laughed," I said. "That's all he could do. They were just too ridiculous."

"He laughed at how those preachers operated: With fear and intimidation. The preachers basically said, 'I'm God's representative here on earth, and He wants you to give up your money so my church can continue to operate.' The TV and radio preachers were even more aggressive about money. They said, 'Give it up or you won't get into heaven.'"

"God likes his preachers to live well. At least, that was Flash's conclusion. He figured that was why there were so many preachers around."

"He said that God must dislike Canada, and that's why He put so many preachers there," Sheri said.

"It filled him with a deep admiration for Buddhists," I said.

"He couldn't figure out Christians no matter how hard he tried. Catholics, Baptists, those services with the yelling and screaming in those overheated rooms…he couldn't make any sense of it. How could the Almighty give so much power to those hypocritical holy rollers who expect everyone to live by those impossible rules? Flash said that God was love, but those religious zealots knew nothing about love."

I sighed and smiled. Sheri always had that effect on me.

"I think Flash has a better grasp of all this," I said. "The Big Coach in the Sky is love, and Flash knows it. If a bunch of fools and jackasses want to use Him as a way of stuffing their pockets with other fools' cash, that's *their* problem, not his."

"But Flash wonders how a true, real, loving God could let those fools get away with that nonsense," Sheri said. "Flash believes that the world is evil, corrupt and rotten, and it's incapable of, or unwilling to, rehabilitate itself. That's just how he feels—that the world is sick and doesn't want to get well, period. His way of coping with a sick society is to pretend it's one big joke and laugh at it."

Sheri looked over at me as the Hawaiian breeze blew through her hair. "It's been very difficult for him, you know. Feeling the way he does, and it's always been this way for him."

"Well," I said, "whatever he thinks he's trying to find—himself, God, nirvana, call it what you want—he's going about it the wrong way. If he buggers off to India and goes to the swamis for all the answers to life's biggest questions, he'll just end up more confused than ever." I paused. "I know that he and I are different in many ways, and he's always been a restless sort who's had a hard time finding peace of mind and stability. But he says that God is love, and love, for him, is you, and yet he runs away from the very person who can give him what he wants and needs. I can't figure him out."

Sheri said nothing.

"I don't care," I went on, "about how many books Flash has read or how much Shakespeare he has learned. I don't give a crap about how worldly or sophisticated or tortured he likes to think he is. What I *do* care about is love. It's rarer and more precious than the biggest diamond. So what does he do? He walks away from you. He shouldn't do that when you two are in love."

Sheri looked over at me and smiled. "Art and literature. Bad stuff, eh?"

"Books are just words on paper that some author wrote for himself. Most books get pulped, and that's a good thing. Only my book, when I manage to finish the fucker, will be read by millions and cherished forever."

"What do you think of art? You know, paintings and sculptures?"

I yawned.

Sheri laughed.

"Do you know who artists are?" I asked her rhetorically. "They're people who work alone because nobody else has any use for them.

197

They're pedophiles, perverts and outcasts who paint pictures and make shit out of clay and stone because they can do it by themselves."

"Oh." Then, "I'm so glad we're here together. I'm thirsty. Go get me a Bud."

I did, and we sat together on the beach for a long while, just looking out at the ocean and sky. I thought for a moment of the sharks out there hungry for sea turtles or baby humpback whales but willing to settle for vacationing Canadian football players.

"Did Flash ever," she wanted to know, "tell you that he felt you and I would make a great couple?"

"Hey? You, me, us? Are you kidding?"

"He told me that lots of times," Sheri said. "He said you and I would be quite an item because you would worship me and that's what every woman wanted, even if she didn't know it. To be worshiped. He could never worship anyone because he just wasn't a worshipful person."

"Very nice," I said.

"Don't you worship me?" she asked.

"I think you're a helluva great guy."

"I suppose being worshiped is a good thing," she said. "Tell me what you know about it. Does it come with tons of cool perks?"

I just shrugged.

"I wonder," she said, "if you and I could start making love to each other after a lifetime of just being best buddies or brother and sister or whatever we've been to each other. It's a fascinating question."

"No, it's not."

"Maybe you're right. It wouldn't work out because we'd have too much fun. We would spend all our time laughing and we would never get anything done. Is that about right?"

"Yeah, that's about it."

"We could play games, you know. You could put on a tie and carry a briefcase. You could go out every morning, pretending that you had an office job. But you would go into a bar all day and drink Canadian Comfort over ice. I could get all tricked out as a high-priced chippie and pick you up in that bar. We could negotiate my price and you could try to talk me out of my sinful profession."

"Lovely."

"Or how about this? When we get back to Bayporte, we'll pretend you're an appliance repairman I've called to fix my whatever. I'll meet you at the door nude and we can take it from

there." "Wow."

"Better still, we could pretend we were starring in a porn movie. We could rent a smelly hotel room and fuck each other in front of my Sony Camcorder. We could do one take after another, each one worse than the one before it."

"We could pretend we were making a snuff movie," I said. "I could make like I made you swallow a bottle of Drano at the end."

"Then you could mutilate my body so nobody would ever know I was dead." Sheri paused. "It would take a lot of effort, but I guess you have to do these things to make love work."

"When we get back to Bayporte, Flash will be there," I said.

"Oh, *that* guy? What an asshole."

Sheri got up and walked towards the ocean until the water covered her feet. Then she stood and stared for quite some time.

I do know that, whatever possessed Flash to run off the way he did, the Super Bowl had nothing to do with it. I suppose I should write about the big game now, even though I don't particularly want to do so.

I find it difficult now to believe how anxious we were about the game. We must have set a new record for queasy stomachs and trips to the washroom.

"Remember," Flash said in the locker room, "no matter what happens today, ninety-nine percent of the world couldn't care less."

Nobody laughed.

The Stars, damn their stuck-up asses, won the coin toss and chose to kick, which was a good idea for them. In such a big game, you want to get your defense in there right away to rough up their offense and show them you've come to kick some asses.

Everyone who saw the game from the stands in Great Elizabeth Place or on TV knew how pumped up the Invaders were that day. We slammed into each other and jumped around like a bunch of speed freaks, and it was for real. We weren't just putting on some kind of show.

Rudy Warkentin and I are always the two deep backs on kick returns, in case you believe that nonsense that *Sports Illustrated* or *Canadian Sports* ran about Ed Lowelling having made a huge blunder by putting me back there for the opening kickoff.

I have been returning kickoffs for my whole life in football, in case anyone wants to know. I've probably returned half a dozen for touchdowns, too.

Alas, their kickoff to us was very bad—or very good, depending on your point of view—and it hit the ground and bounced erratically as Rudy tried to pick it up. He may have gotten a fingertip or two on it before being pummeled by two or three Stars on our five-yard line.

I remember not thinking much at all as the football danced and rolled towards the end zone and I scrambled over to pick it up, knowing that those Stars who had just nailed my teammate were coming over to hit me, too.

Well, if you saw it live or on TV, you saw Jethro Payne slam into me as soon as I touched the ball, and, yes, that hit hurt every bit as much as you guessed. It also knocked loose the football, which Jethro picked up and trotted into the end zone for six points. But he made me laugh when, after spiking the ball and wagging his ass at my thousands of booing fans, he came over to help me up and spoke into my ringing ears.

He said, "Don't forget to put *that* into your bestselling book."

That humiliating turnover and Jethro's touchdown stripped us of most of our confidence for most of the first half. Hell, we didn't start to get our heads together until halftime.

Vernon Braithwaite, for quite some time, seemed unable to comprehend that he was supposed to throw a pass, hand off the ball or run with it himself, rather than just stand there and let a stuck-up Star sack him.

Flash got as open as a starlet's stuff on one down after another; Vernon, if he didn't get sacked, threw the ball so far past Flash that the play-by-play boys in the broadcast booth nearly caught it.

After Vernon threw his fifth consecutive incompletion, Flash jogged back to us and said, "Next time, I'm just going to keep running till I reach Starbucks. Anyone want a latte?"

Vernon just said, "Let's do it, ladies. Let's take it to them and win this thing."

Vernon got poor protection, I must admit, or none at all. On some plays, our offensive linemen—the guys who were there to make sure Vernon got rid of the ball before the Stars touched him—seemed unsure which Stars they were supposed to block, so they blocked nobody at all, and as soon as Vernon got the snap, the stuck-up Stars came at him like screaming banshees.

"Motherfuckers," Vernon muttered as he got up off the ground, refusing the assistance of the Stars who had put him down. "What happened to my guys? Did they all go to Starbucks with Flash?"

No, we hadn't taken off for lattes. In fact, the stuck-up Stars were playing us the usual way, just as Flash and I had predicted. Painless, quick as a fox and solid as a locomotive, covered the secondary with one eye on Flash, regardless of how deep my pal went.

Clearly, the stuck-up Stars considered Flash their biggest threat, and that the best way of stopping him was to keep pressure on Vernon.

The Stars' defensive line moved and fidgeted constantly, causing us much anxiety. When Vernon stood behind our center and started calling signals, Jethro Payne would move in closer because he knew he freaked out Vernon, and his strategy caused a few bad snaps and delay-of-game penalties when Vernon decided to call an audible for John Kerluke to get in motion and block for me, but Kerluke yelled, "Check," meaning he couldn't hear the audible, and kept yelling "Check" until the Stars all burst out laughing and the referee gave us a five-yard penalty.

Also, I hated hearing Jethro Payne as he spoke personally to me from the line of scrimmage.

"Come on, Red Crossley, get that football and come say hi to Painless. I got a little something for you."

Or he would say, "Vernon Braithwaite, I see you. Do you see me? Painless gonna come by and give you a kiss."

Only a superstar athlete, from whom everyone expects everything, can understand how intimidated and humiliated we felt for the first half of that Super Bowl. Yes, we all played badly that first half. All the sports media accused Flash of suffering from an acute case of cockiness that first half, and maybe they're right.

Many have said that was why Flash dropped a few very catchable passes from Vernon, and fumbled the one catch he did make, which a stuck-up Star quickly picked up and ran back for a touchdown.

Flash, in fact, dropped one ball because he knew he had an easy touchdown and felt so eager to get into the end zone that he just started off a moment too soon and couldn't quite secure the football in the crook of his arm.

As the pigskin bounced away, Flash returned to the huddle and said, "It's not much fun catching a ball if it's too easy."

Vernon said, "Let's get busy, ladies. Let's win this thing and order our rings."

Flash dropped another pass because a few stuck-up Stars converged on Vernon, who panicked and threw ball well over Flash's head. When Flash went up to try to make the impossible catch, two or three Stars waited for him to come back down and hit him at the same time, making the ball pop out of his hands and bounce out of bounds.

But, if you're a member of the sports media, you probably think that if your name is Flash Gortton and you collect those monster paychecks, you have no excuse for failing to make those miraculous catches.

When Flash caught that pass, and then fumbled the ball, in the first quarter, the turnover happened because Painless drilled him hard enough to rattle his teeth.

Flash caught the ball practically on his shoulder pad—just a wimpy little screen pass intended for maybe five yards—and Painless nailed him so hard that Sheri swore everyone in Great Elizabeth Place could hear them go *Bam!*

The ball popped up into the air for what seemed forty-five minutes and descended into the hands of Stars linebacker Rick Single of Georgia Tech, who practically waltzed in for a touchdown.

The bastard could have stopped for pie and coffee on his way to score and still entered the end zone untouched. I'd given him a few seconds of feeble chase, and Vernon, who often throws himself to the ground to avoid being touched by a would-be tackler, simply watched and shook his head as Single scored.

Sheri says that after we began trailing by two touchdowns, the crowd—mostly Invaders fans dressed in garish team apparel—grew quiet and glum despite the generous amount of time left for us to make a comeback.

Lord Larry, according to his daughter, shouted alternately at Painless and Eddie Lowelling.

"Get him! Get him!" Lord Larry kept yelling at Painless. "Hit him low! Take him out of the bloody game or we're finished!"

Art Jones, sitting next to Sheri, just sighed and said, "I knew it was too good to be true. We kept hoping and praying our guys would win it all at home, but I guess some things just weren't meant to be."

Sheri said that Jeter Davis, who looked as if he hadn't slept in a month, just stared morosely at the gridiron and mumbled to himself about how much money he had lost betting on the Invaders.

The pessimism in the stands hardly compared to the despair on the field. We were close to giving up when L.T. Briggs wrapped Ralph Stefani into a bear hug and stripped him of the football, which we recovered but could not convert into anything more than a field goal. Still, we had something on the scoreboard and, therefore, something to feel confident about.

I objected to our field goal attempt, mainly because we were on their two-yard line and Flash or I could have gotten the ball into the end zone, but Ed Lowelling pointed out our poor track record on conversions. So Ed prevailed, and those Invaders fans who booed and threw debris at Vernon Braithwaite once he left the field should be ashamed of themselves.

I know that Eddie made the decision to kick a field goal because Flash and I stood there and listened as Eddie and Vernon talked it out. I told Eddie I wanted Vernon to hand off to me so I could leap, Jim Brown-style, over everyone for six points instead of three. We were down by so many points that three seemed like zero.

But Eddie said, "Red, Superman himself couldn't jump over that pile of bodies, so we'll just have to take the three."

Vernon said he wanted to try for six anyway, but Eddie said,

"Yeah, and if we fuck that up and end up with nothing, those stuck-up bastards will really start looking down their noses at us."

Then Flash said, "They're laughing at us right now."

Even now, I'm totally convinced I could have done that Jim Brown jump and gotten the pigskin into the end zone for six, but we did as Eddie ordered as got a whole three points up on the scoreboard.

We trailed twenty-one to three as we went into the locker room at halftime. Every player swore, pounded the walls or threw his helmet.

"Candyasses!" yelled L.T. Briggs. "We're nothing but a bunch of motherfuckin' candyasses!" He threw down his helmet and screamed, *"No more bullshit!"*

We went in every direction, all of us muttering; some guys went to get a Coke or Pepsi from the tub sitting full of iced cans, while others went to the washroom.

"Vernon Braithwaite!" L.T. called out. "Braithwaite! You know what your problem is today? You're asleep! Wake fuckin' up, candyass!"

Vernon sat at his locker, sorting through some items, and let on that he did not hear what had just been said.

L.T. had a bit more to say.

"I'm the boss of the defense, and my defense has held them to one pissy little pass completion, and the only reason they got it is 'cause our boy who was coverin' their boy didn't cover their boy good enough. Hey, boy! Where are you? Come on out here!"

"Boy" is what L.T. Briggs calls you whenever he can't remember your name, which is often. Alex Hamilton, the boy to whom L.T. was referring,

Alex said, "What you want, big man?"

"Boy, you get your ass up here in front of everybody and promise us all that you ain't gonna let any of them candyasses out there catch any more passes if you can help it!"

Alex Hamilton ambled into the center of the room and shrugged. "I'll fuck 'em. I'll be all over 'em."

"No more bullshit from them motherfuckin' Stars!" L.T. screamed. "We got one more half to show 'em who's boss! Let's do it!"

Around Vernon Braithwaite's locker, a few of us loiterers started getting a bit pissed off, and I suspect it had something to do with what Flash said.

"Are you trying to lose this game?" Flash asked him.

Vernon snarled at him.

"How much will you win if we lose, Vern? That's the only reason I can think of to explain why you're playing such shitty football today."

"And what about *you*, superstar? You've been forgetting where you're supposed to be when I'm ready to throw you the ball. Try getting your mind off snatch for a little while, OK?"

"I can't catch your passes when they end up in the stands or out in the parking lot. That's called 'out of bounds.'"

"Listen up," interjected Pol Pott. "We can't win this game when we're talking like that. They don't have to worry about defeating us because we're defeating ourselves. We can beat them if we pull together."

"Piss off, Pol," I said. "You haven't done a thing all bloody day."

"We're gonna do it," Pol said. "We're gonna take over this game and become the Super Bowl champions of the world."

"Yeah," retorted Flash, "and I'm going to have the biggest, fanciest condo on Mars."

"Everyone," I said, "shut your ass up and let's try to figure out how we're going to win this damn thing."

"A good running game would help," Vernon said, directing his remark at me. "You haven't exactly looked like Gayle Sayers today."

"Gotta maintain a positive mental attitude," Pol Pott said. "Gotta believe we can do it."

"Maybe," said Flash, "we should call Joe Montana and pull him out of retirement so he could get us out of this mess. Anyone know his cell phone number?"

"Enough bickering," I said. "We have to remember that we're a team and we have two whole quarters to get back into this game."

Vernon said, "I think I can make some touchdown passes if my teammates will give me some protection."

"We all need a positive mental attitude," Pol Pott said.

Suddenly, L.T. Briggs shouted, "How come everyone's talking and not the coaches? Where the fuck is Lowelling? I bet he's ashamed of us after seeing us play like a bunch of candyasses."

L.T. had a point. No coach was in the locker room. The only sign we had that a coach had been there and knew the score, literally and figuratively, was a message written on the big white board.

The message was: NEVER GIVE UP.

None of us had noticed it till that moment because we had all entered the locker room swearing and blaming each other for the lopsided score. Also, we didn't actually get around to talking to each other about the best way to play in the second half. Personally, I just decided to play a bit harder and hope that we would enjoy some divine intervention.

We finally saw Eddie, he merely came in, said something about how the rest of the game was ours to win or lose, then he left the room.

I'm not sure if divine intervention happened to us in the second half, but Lady Luck damn sure did help us out. They kicked off, we got the ball on our own twenty yard line and we *knew* we had to show them we still had plenty of fight.

We needed, of course, to get an efficient drive started, one that would culminate in a touchdown. Another dumb-ass little field goal would do us very little good.

Vernon called the logical play, a handoff to me. I got eight yards and was not creamed by Painless. The stuck-up Stars clearly did not expect good ol' Red to carry the ball that time, and they sort of just stood there looking at me as I hustled past and through them.

"Positive mental attitude," said Pol Pott in the huddle. "We can do it if we *think* we can do it."

As you surely know if you watched the game, our drive wasn't pretty, but we took it. A pass-interference call helped us when one of the stuck-up Stars got all tangled up with Flash, and it happened again when one of their guys interfered with Jimmy Svec. It also helped us that when Svec fumbled, the referee, for some stupid but wonderful reason, blew his whistle and called the play dead right before a stuck-up Star could recover it.

"We got things going our way," Vernon said. "Flash, you go long and I'll get it to you this time."

"Promise?" Flash asked.

Vernon got the pass to Flash, sort of.

The online services published many images of Flash in the air, limbs contorted almost acrobatically, magically making the catch and getting us to about the stuck-up Stars' thirty yard line.

I suppose this was the first time we felt we had made some progress against the Stars, and we were determined to put six on the board.

Vernon handed off to me, and I got four yards before being pushed out of bounds. Then Vernon, flushed out of the pocket, scrambled for several more yards. He called for a timeout.

I went with Vernon to confer on the sidelines with Eddie, and for the very first time I could hear the noise from the crowd. Great Elizabeth Place, a huge stadium packed with people, overwhelmed me as never before. One moment, I wanted to vomit; the next, I wanted to run home to Mum. After that, I forgot about vomiting and Mum and started listening to Eddie and Hose.

"You're doing something right," said Eddie.

"We're holding and doing other illegal things but they're getting penalized for it." Vernon grinned.

"Tell you what," Eddie said. "From now on, our game is you, Red and Flash. The rest of those guys aren't jackshit. We need six points each time we have possession or we're fucked."

Vernon and I returned to the field, he called a handoff to me and I gained a few yards, and on the next play I got a few more after he pitched the ball to me.

Then Eddie Lowelling, that simpleton, called a timeout that we didn't need, and he told Vernon and me what we already knew. "OK,

it's fourth and goal, and we're at their one-foot line. When

this happens, we go with our best player and his best play. That's you,

Red, and we need you to do one of them Jim Brown jumps over

everyone and get that football into the end zone. Think you can do

it?"

"I think I can, I think I can." I sounded like The Little Football

Player that Could.

Many football fans will think of that play as the biggest of the

game, just the way they thought of Dwight Clark's huge touchdown

reception in 1982 versus the Dallas Cowboys. I *do* know that my

touchdown run instantly became the obsession of the sports media

and Twitter users and got countless views on YouTube.

It is always a difficult call when the rusher leaps over the

mountain of bodies on the goal line and then falls backwards. The

referees must decide: did the ball carrier break the plane of the end

zone? Once Vernon handed me the ball, I jumped onto Pol Pott's

back and sprang to the top of the wall of men. Painless, among

others, stood waiting to give me a kiss hello.

Plus, the referee had to decide if I had scored the touchdown, which would have ended the play, before Painless popped me a Mike Tyson shot and the ball came loose as I fell backwards. The loose football, of course, triggered the fistfight that looked for a few minutes as if it would last all afternoon.

Anyway, one referee threw up his hands to indicate a touchdown, while a second official pointed downfield, to indicate that the stuck-up Stars had recovered the football. A third wanted a timeout as half a dozen or so Invaders and as many Stars started punching the bejesus out of each other.

Both benches emptied as the players joined the fight much the way baseball and hockey players do when things get violent on the playing field. Whistles blew and referees tried feebly to separate big, strong combatants as they mixed it up like stuntmen in a Bruce Lee movie. I didn't get into the fracas, and neither did Painless, because we both knew the folly of getting hurt and being taken out of the game. We grabbed hold of each other, pretended to fight, and laughed our asses off instead.

Once the fight ended—and it ended because the referees finally figured out that the fisticuffs were happening at Great Elizabeth Place on Super Bowl Sunday, in front of a sold-out crowd and the rest of the football-loving world on TV while the refs were supposed to maintain order—the referees took a nice long time with the instant replay, to make a definitive determination about our touchdown. They couldn't do that, but they gave us the six points anyway.

So it became 21-10, and we began to feel optimistic. Sheri said that people in the stands shared our surge of confidence. Her father went bananas over the plays Eddie insisted on calling, but he seemed pacified by the touchdown. She told me that her father remarked, "It looks like we have a chance of winning this thing, but I don't know how much stamina and resiliency our boys have left."

Did I break the plane of the end zone? I believe so, but obviously there's no way I can prove it, no matter how many times I watch it on YouTube. Psychologically, that drive gave us a huge boost. We discovered some of their weaknesses and vulnerabilities, and that huge fistfight between the two teams showed that we were grown men and professional football players, not just a bunch of wimps to be pushed around and scored against. Also, 21-10, in an NFL game, with plenty of time to go, seemed like a very surmountable challenge.

Alas, we lost of some of our confidence when they received the kickoff and, on three plays ended up at our goal line. Miraculously,

L.T. Briggs, inadequately blocked, stripped the ball from Ralph Stefani and carried it for nearly five yards before he, the slowest of players, was tackled by five Stars.

We all congratulated L.T. as he came off the field.

"Them candyasses ain't won nothin' yet," he said.

L.T.'s strip, in my opinion, certainly qualified as one of the game's most significant plays, even if the online news services essentially ignored it. if the Stars had scored then, we would have been goners.

L.T. had gotten us ball, but we couldn't do anything with it and had to punt it away. Jimmy Svec then redeemed himself by recovering the punt they fumbled. As you probably remember, the ball took a truly insane bounce and seemed to roll forever as Jimmy chased it like a Klansman pursuing a black guy in 1962 Mississippi. I felt deeply gratified when the referee called it ours on the stuck-up Stars' twelve yard line.

I knew that if we had a few more lucky plays like that we would reduce our deficit even more.

In the huddle, Vernon Braithwaite called for Flash to sprint into the end zone and wait for the pass. Flash did just that, and Painless must have been expecting me to come barreling through with the ball because Flash caught it in the end zone uncovered, and we had six more on the board just like that.

When the fourth quarter began, we clearly had a chance of winning because the score was 21-17. Sheri said that the Invaders fans were on the verge of going into a frenzy, and that Art Jones had run over to give Murphy O'Grady a big hug. Then he high-fived everyone he could reach and pumped his fist at everyone in Great Elizabeth Place.

"Way to go!" Art shouted. "We're gonna win this bloody thing! We're gonna win it yet!"

Then Lord Larry said, "We've got them! They're choking! It's just a matter of time! Our first Super Bowl! Hooray!"

Sheri said her father quieted down the moment Jethro Payne picked off a Vernon Braithwaite pass and sprinted off for a Stars touchdown.

Painless' touchdown sickened all of us like a punch to the solar plexus. We certainly would have just traipsed off to our bench and wept or puked, or both, if our teammate Bobby Garcia hadn't caught their kickoff and run it right into their end zone to get us right back into the contest.

I don't care that the Internet sources showed Bobby stepping out of bounds at least twice, but the main thing is that once Bobby entered the end zone the referee signaled touchdown, and we were back in this thing.

I still blush when I think of how I ran behind him into the end zone and, like some kind of flamboyant faggot, leapt on him, took him down and practically kissed him.

Sheri said her father couldn't believe what Bobby had done; Lord Larry, according to her, said, "I would have guessed that little bugger wasn't much good for anything except manning a taco stand."

Art Jones and Jeter Davis both wept into their cupped hands.

I would love to tell you that we had finally figured out how to beat the stuck-up Stars. I really would.

I would also love to tell you that we had gotten our second wind as we battled the stuck-up Stars and that freakin' time clock, and that we were sharp and poised and overcame ourselves in order to overcome our opponents.

Here in Hawaii, I've spent plenty of time mentally reviewing that fourth quarter in Bayporte as I've sat on the beach and gazed out at the magnificent Pacific Ocean and Hawaiian sky as Sheri strolled about in her bikini.

Truthfully, all I can remember of those final minutes of the Super Bowl is that I was so stupefied by exhaustion I could barely move.

In our huddles, Vernon sounded like a mental case. "OK, ladies, we're running out of time, we gotta get it together and move the ball forward, let's get it on, let's get it done."

I heard Vernon call the same audibles, but now they made no sense to me. He got the snap and I ran forward and got hit by someone in a Stars uniform. I suppose I ran in the right direction, because nobody yelled at me afterwards.

At some point, Flash said to me, "You feeling OK, Red?" I remember Vernon saying, "Of course he's OK. He's about to win the Super Bowl."

Vernon came up with some kind of call when we had fourth down and a couple to go on our own forty. We had to go for the first down, of course, because time was running out, and if we punted, we probably would never regain possession of the ball.

I had no idea of what Vernon would do. Maybe hand off the ball to me? Throw a pass to Flash? Maybe keep the ball and just run like hell with it, a la Joe Montana? He would probably just do whatever the hell was necessary to get that first down. Vernon himself didn't know what he would do, and the stuck-up Stars certainly didn't know, either.

"Ladies," Vernon said in the huddle, "this is the ballgame. Everyone get open."

"Just throw the fucker long," said Flash, "and I'll catch it."

If Vernon had thrown an adequate pass, of course, Flash would have scored a touchdown for the simple reason that Flash had no coverage whatsoever. Unfortunately, Vernon threw a dreadful pass that Flash caught only because of his considerable agility, and nobody could quite figure out how he managed to keep both feet in bounds as he fell.

I am still amazed that I carried the ball half a dozen consecutive times after that, and I say amazed because I just don't remember any of those carries. I especially don't remember slamming into Painless and knocking him flat on his ass. They tell me that his teammates had to help him off the field. Imagine that.

I sat on the bench and tried to get my head in order. I looked up at the game clock and saw that we had six seconds left in regulation time. Then I gazed up around the ninety thousand or so people who had crowded into Great Elizabeth Place and realized that I couldn't hear anything even though they clearly were making plenty of noise. It was the strangest thing; I thought for a little while that I had gone deaf.

They tell me that I jumped onto Pol Pott's massive back and hurled myself over everyone and landed in the end zone on my head to win the game. Frankly, I don't remember any of it; I think I may have fallen asleep during that play. I have only the vaguest recollection of being carried off the field the way a sick child might be carried to the emergency room.

I remember hearing Jeter Davis slapping my helmet and shouting, "You beat 'em, Red! You beat those stuck-up Stars!"

Art Jones rushed up to me, tears streaming down his face, and if I hadn't been wearing a helmet, he probably would have tried to kiss me.

Eddie Lowelling shook my head and yelled into my face, "That's professionalism, Red!"

Lord Larry pressed a wad of hundred-dollar bills into my hand and exclaimed, "Just a little something for you, Red! To show you that the whole bloody province of Great Elizabeth appreciates what you've just done for us!"

In the locker room, after most of the whooping and hollering had quieted down and the players had grown tired of dousing each other with champagne, Flash came up to me and shook my hand. "You took 'em down, Red," is all he said.

Honestly, as delighted as I am to be a member of the Super Bowl-winning Bayporte Invaders, I don't consider the final score to be much of a drumming. Furthermore, if we played the Stars again next month, they would probably take us, and by a much more lopsided score. The sportswriters did the right thing when they voted Painless as Player of the Game. Sure, I would have enjoyed getting the trophy and all the other goodies, but Painless certainly deserved the award.

I noticed that the sports media completely ignored the face that Painless came over to our locker room and congratulated us on our victory. After he had cleaned himself up and put on his street clothes so that nobody would recognize him, he came by and shook our hands, which I thought was very big of him.

"Good game you played," he said to us. "I thought we had you in a death grip but you got out of it."

I smiled and nodded. "Could have gone either way. Things

happened in that game that probably shouldn't have happened." He

shook his head. "It turned out the way it was supposed to."

Painless said that he and I should try to get to know each other a little bit better, since we were always flying from one city to another and would probably end up on the same flight now and again. I said sure, yeah, we would definitely do that.

"You won the big one, guy," he said as he left. "Numbers don't lie."

As Painless left, I thought he was a stand-up guy and hoped he would have a Super Bowl ring of his own, as long as I wasn't playing against him.

I have a feeling that I've come to the end of this book for the simple reason that I've run out of things to say. I'd like to give Flash another chance to show up here in Hawaii before I have to get busy and board another flight back to the Mainland.

I really hate not knowing where Flash is or when he'll turn up. I probably sound like a Jewish mother, but that's just how I am.

Maybe he'll just walk in wearing an aloha shirt, cutoffs and sandals and pretend nothing's the matter. Maybe he'll do that before time runs out and Sheri and I have to catch that flight back home and fulfill our many obligations.

I will write some more for you, my dear reader, after I've gone back home, hooked up with my collaborator and let him shape all this text into a readable book.

Right now I need to take a swim in the Pacific Ocean because we'll be leaving soon and I don't really know when we'll be coming back here. The rest of the world just can't seem to get enough of Red Crossley and Sheri Rawson.

Hello, my fellow Canadians. As your Prime Minister, I speak to you tonight about a matter of the highest importance. Certain highly placed officials in our government have alerted me to the fact that some of our professional athletes are smoking marijuana and drinking alcoholic beverages.

I have also discovered that poverty and unrest exist in some of our major cities. I have learned this sad truth via the Internet.

I consider this highly unfortunate and wish to inform you that if

227

they do not stop soon I am going to fly somewhere warm and sunny and play some golf to get my mind off these depressing domestic issues.

Now, let's deal with something cheerful. I want to you say hello to my friend and fellow proud Canadian, Red Crossley. Red, say hello to Canada.

How's it goin', eh?

Red, you were the star of the Super Bowl, am I

right? One of them.

You did a great job, Red. You made us all

proud. It's nice to be appreciated.

Red, you are an athlete worshiped all over the word, and especially by our young people here in Canada. Since so many people think so highly of you, I want to ask you if you think it's a good idea for people to drink alcohol or use illegal drugs. There's the camera, Red. All of Canada is watching, so please just tell them what you think.

This camera? The one with the red light on?

Yes, Red. Tell your country what you think.

Well, I'm Red Crossley and I have plenty to say about the use of recreational drugs. I don't think it's good to use drugs if you're all by yourself and you just want to get stoned out of your

mind— Uh, Red—

If you want to get stoned, I think you're much better off to get your drugs from a reliable dealer rather than buying some stepped-on garbage from an unethical street dealer.

Red—

I have something else on my mind. I heard the other day that masturbating while you watch online porn is bad for your health. I totally disagree. Lots of very nice people masturbate to online porn and it hasn't hurt them one bit except for sore hands.

Red!

Well, you asked and I answered. I gotta go. I have some porn on my laptop and a boner that just won't go down.

Me again. Forgive the page you've just read; I was having some fun, just goofing off at the expense of our Prime Minister and my public image. The truth is, I was trying to amuse my very wonderful, special and gorgeous lifelong friend, Sheri Rawson.

We're back from vacation and taking it easy in our apartment overlooking rainy Bayporte. I'm sitting in my favorite chair with my MacBook Pro on my lap and a Canadian Comfort over ice on the table next to me.

Sheri sits across the living room in her tight Levi's and T-shirt concealing one magnificent pair of blonde Canadian titties. When I look up from the computer screen and stare at her titties, she notices and flips me off.

Great tits, no class.

Sheri's gone now, off to Northern Lights Mall, probably, to buy herself some shoes to add to the hundred pairs she already owns. Northern Lights' management markets itself as western Canada's most expensive shopping mall, as if that's anything to brag about. But it's good that Sheri has taken off for a few hours so that I can continue writing this uniquely insightful book.

I'm far behind schedule on this project. Spring is imminent, and I feel fine as I walk around town, knowing that we won that damned Super Bowl after all and nobody can take that away from us.

We haven't heard from Flash since he sent us those emails during our stay in Hawaii, and a part of me is starting to believe that he really has disappeared forever. Sheri says he may return, but not until many years have passed. This has been our longest-ever separation, so maybe Sheri is right, but deep down I don't believe that the next time I see him we will be a couple of senile old men.

I am confused about Flash's fascination with wandering the planet and meeting odd people and eating weird foods. Flash probably doesn't know, either, and doesn't expect to figure himself out in this lifetime.

Sheri and I have to go our separate ways, temporarily. I wanted her to keep me company as I went on the road to meet with the media and did the banquet circuit to give speeches. Sheri said she wanted to get out of Bayporte for a while so Lord Larry and Lady Joy wouldn't bug her to death about every little thing.

"I'm up for a couple of gigs in Toronto and New York," she said. "Mostly feminine hygiene stuff. How come they always pick me to be the face of 'chick on the rag'?"

I'll be going to different cities, too, of course, and in some ways it should be fun. Look up some friends and acquaintances, eat some authentic foreign cuisine, hit on some foreign women, get good and drunk in funky bars.

"We've spent our lives trying to escape Bayporte," Sheri said. "But we always come back. Why?"

"Because it's our home and native land," I said. "I'm eager to go over my book with Snoop. It's starting to become a hassle. I want to see it published, shamelessly promote it, gloat when it becomes a major bestseller and then get on with the other things in my life. We could do our traveling together, you know."

Sheri shook her head. "You do your thing and I'll do mine. I have plenty of things happening, and traveling alone enables me to meet many interesting people and join subversive organizations."

"I see. You're the daughter of a rich man, yet you are opposed to wealth and the people who control it."

"I'm just a walking contradiction, partly truth and partly fiction," she said.

I met up with Snoop back in Bayporte to take a first look at my manuscript. I felt smug as he read what I had written and I expected him to love every word of it.

"I want to know more about your evening at Combat Zone," he

said. "Your readers will want to know more, too. That's the kind of stuff that makes readers turn pages—you know, getting high in that nightclub, feeling up the server, looking up the dancers' skirts because they're not wearing panties."

"Yeah, whatever." I yawned.

"There's quite a little bit of profanity, but I guess that's OK. The publishers won't mind."

"Those words are in the dictionary, you know."

"Two people are very eager to read your book," Snoop said. "They are: Lord Larry and your Uncle Joey. Let's not disappoint them."

"I agree. But each time I sit down to write, I come away with the feeling that I could have done better. I'm just never satisfied with it."

"Well, I'll go through it and help you as much as I can, but you need to remember that you need to get this thing to the publisher while Red Crossley is still trending on Google and the people out there still give a shit about what you have to say."

I met up with my Uncle Andy at Harry's Billiards, a downtown Bayporte pool hall from the 1950s, as anachronistic as jukebox or a drive-in. We stood and watched as old men chalked up cues and racked up balls in a city where most people were young and played computer games.

"This place won't be here in a few years, and neither will I," Uncle Andy said amid the clatter of colliding balls and grunting, muttering pensioners.

"The condo developers are checking it out. With this location, I'm sure they'll make a few million. Same goes for that nightclub down the street, the Igloo. Can you believe that place used to be a big, popular ice skating rink? People's idea of entertainment has changed."

He introduced me to his friends. "This is my nephew, Red Crossley. I won some money when the Invaders won the Super Bowl."

His friends barely looked in my direction and muttered hello, but one said, "I don't know for sure, but I think someone paid off those bloody refs."

Uncle Andy and I sat at the snack bar and sipped some coffee.

"Red," he said, "let me tell you how proud I am of you for winning that Super Bowl. The Invaders got themselves into an impossible predicament and said, 'Here, Red, take the ball and win this game for us.' And you rose to the occasion. That shows real character."

I smirked. "You won that big bet, too. I'm sure that made you feel good, hey?"

He waved this off. "Winning the bet was nice, but it didn't mean all that much. Winning the game meant something. Can you imagine? By some fluke, Bayporte gets chosen as this year's Super Bowl location, and the Invaders end up playing in it! Against the Toronto Stars, our big rival! Can you imagine what would have happened if the Invaders had lost the Super Bowl? There would have been riots."

I nodded and sipped my coffee. We watched as a few guys wandered in who seemed to have more dollars than sense, and Uncle Andy decided they needed to be fleeced.

As I left, he said to me, "Remember, Andy: 'Being Number One is lots of fun, but being Number Two just won't do.'"

Dinner with Lord Larry and Lady Joy, of course, was an obligation I could not postpone forever. So I met them at the West Shore Country Club, hoping they would limit our get-together to themselves and me, but they asked some of their friends to join us. Rory Gilsenan, one of Lord Larry's Yukon partners, sat at our table with his wife, Ronaye. They all congratulated me on the Super Bowl and guessed that I was happy to be back in Bayporte, if only for the time being.

They shared horror stories of big-city American servers, taxi drivers, hotel personnel and store clerks.

"My thing," said Rory, "is to go there, do my thing and leave as soon as I can."

Not knowing what else to do, I just sat there and smiled and nodded, as if I felt the way he did.

Lord Larry asked me about Flash.

"Flash's dad hasn't heard from him since they spoke right after the Super Bowl. Sheri says he's just run off somewhere to 'find himself.' What the hell is that supposed to mean?"

I shrugged. "Just what it sounds like. Flash has gone off to find himself. When Flash finds Flash, they'll both come home."

Lord Larry made a face. "Ha, ha. He's going all over the world with no particular destination in mind, eh? That's a good way to get yourself killed. The world is a dangerous, unstable place. He's a fool to be so reckless."

"When do you think Flash will come home?" Lord Larry asked.

"When he's ready to do that. He's got the resources to stay away for a good long time."

"And what is Sheri supposed to do while Flash is somewhere out there gazing at his navel?" Lord Larry wanted to know.

"Sheri is supposed to be unconditionally supportive," I said.

They all looked at me, and at each other, wondering if I was simply making a joke.

"That's bloody lovely," Lord Larry said finally. "Rory, how would you like to run your business that way?"

"I wouldn't be in business for very long," replied Rory.

Lady Joy sighed and said, "How I wish Sheri was married and had children. It would be terrific if she lived out here in West Shore and had a traditional lifestyle. The three of you have such weird lives. You spend all your time on flights, in airports and taxis and hotels. It's so pointless." Then, looking past us and noticing a mirror, she smoothed back her hair.

Lord Larry said, "Some people know how to live right but other people don't."

I told him I agreed, then excused myself and thanked them for dinner.

"You be sure and tell Sheri," said Rory, "that she's much too beautiful a woman to be flying here and there, doing this and that. Tell her that here in Bayporte we have plenty of eligible males with plenty to offer her, if you know what I mean."

"Yessir, I'll tell her what you said." I could imagine what she would say in retort. "And if you see Flash before I do, be sure to tell him that the Invaders have drafted a wide receiver who can catch everything in the air that doesn't require a trip to the doctor."

Lord Larry suddenly decided to walk me out of the country club. He put his arm around my shoulders. Some people at other tables waved me over for handshakes and cell phone pictures.

"This man," Lord Larry said of me, "was born and raised here in Bayporte. And now he's won us our very first Super Bowl. Isn't he something?"

At the lobby, he took me aside and half-whispered, "Red, as you know, I have plenty of money and power. If you and Sheri like, I can put some of my resources towards finding Flash and bringing him home. The world isn't that big a place, and with computers and modern technology, well, the private eyes could catch up with him fast enough. Just a thought."

I smiled and shook my head. Flash, I assured him, was a grown man who was doing what he needed to do. He would return to us when he felt ready to do so, period.

"Seriously, Red," Lord Larry said, his face now grave, "if Flash is in some sort of trouble...I know he likes to smoke pot, and they can be very brutal overseas with foreigners who are caught with drugs. Remember Schapelle Corby, the Aussie who got caught with hashish or something in her bags in Bali? They gave her about twenty years! She won't be released until twenty-seventeen! We don't want anything bad to happen to Flash, of course, so just remember that I know people in all the centers of power. I know the Prime Minister and even lots of people in Washington, too. If Flash got busted, I could have some very important people get him out of trouble."

"Good to know," I said as I walked out the door.

"Very important people," he repeated.

Carol's Place, the new name of an old business, used to be a bikers' hangout called the Lookout, in Cornwall, a suburb of

Bayporte. Located near the Tyson River, the Lookout, according to legend, served as an ideal spot to kill someone because the killer could simply dump his victim's body into the river and its ferocious currents could hide the body forever.

For decades, the Lookout appeared to be what Bayporters had always called a scary place. If you could see its garish neon sign, you were in the wrong part of town. Gangs met and did business there; sometimes things nasty and they shot each other; almost as bad, the cops lucked out, seizing large amounts of cocaine and heroin and making arrests. Near the new millennium, the Lookout's owner, an Arab now sick of all the notoriety, sold his business to someone, who in turn sold it to someone else. Now, as Carol's Place, no longer that shady, infamous criminals' den, it attracted many moderately well-paid blue-collar workers who came in to drink beer and complain of *ennui*.

I got there well before Snoop did, so I ordered a Canadian Comfort over ice and sat at the bar. Nobody recognized me, not even the bartender, and I felt disappointed. Maybe they just didn't expect Red Crossley, Super Bowl badass, to walk into this old, dumpy workingman's joint under the bridge and by the river. The bartender said her name was Brandi. She told me she had a certificate to provide healthcare or something, and that this bartending stuff was getting very old, very fast.

Carol's Place had many tables, most of them occupied by women who looked as if they could be receptionists at Cornwall's ubiquitous dental or medical centers, or maybe they were low-level bank officers. Some guys sat around, too, looking like sales associates or assistant managers at the warehouses or huge furniture stores nearby; Cornwall had acquired a reputation as the only relatively affordable place in the Greater Bayporte Area.

A couple of guys seemed to be checking out my leather jacket, which probably cost more than they earned in a whole month, but they said nothing to me. I wonder what kind of mischief I would have gotten into here around 1975 to 1985, when the Hells Angels and their brethren made this their second home, and surely would have said something to a pretty-boy sports star like me who had come in alone for a quiet beer.

As soon as Snoop arrived, he said, "Let's go to the private section." He meant one of the isolated booths at the back.

"Nobody worth looking at comes in until later," he said. "But if you see someone you find acceptable, speak up. Until then, we just get gooned."

We drank and talked about my book. He wanted to break it into sections, remove this anecdote and put that one in another section. "Also," he said, "just tone down the language here and there." He paused. "How close are you to completing it?"

"I suppose I'll know when I'm done. I've already said most of what I thought was worth saying." Then, "You know that Flash Gortton is running around everywhere. He sent us a few emails indicating that he will never return. I'll wait and see if he comes back, because that would be a great way of ending the book. Otherwise, I'll just end up with Flash's disappearance."

"Got any idea of what he's doing?" Snoop asked.

"Oh, I think he's doing that free-spirited hippie thing everyone was into in the Sixties. He told me was sick of football and wanted to relieve himself of all responsibilities, so he's buggered off to roam and contemplate."

Snoop ordered us a couple of fresh Canadian Comforts over ice.

"How is Sheri coping with Flash's recent behavior?" he asked me.

"Oh, she's coping. She's got all the money, looks and brains in the

world. She's going to sit around waiting for her old man to come back until she gets sick of it, then she's going to get on with her own life. She knows plenty of people here, plus Toronto and New York. She keeps busy. She gets offers. If Flash doesn't show up, she'll meet someone else. She's a Rawson; she refuses to let people make a fool of her."

Brandi came by with two more Canadian Comforts over ice.

"Have you met this man?" Snoop asked her as he pointed to me.

"Are you Red Crossley?" she asked. "I thought it was you when you came in. But then I asked myself, 'Why would Red Crossley be in this part of town?'"

"Well, I have to be *somewhere*, don't I?"

Brandi whipped out her cell phone and I posed with her for a picture.

"My kids will be so excited that I met you! I bet they'll piss their pants!"

"That excited, eh?" I said.

Snoop said, "Brandi, if anyone decent-looking comes in, be sure to ask her if she'd like to meet Red Crossley."

"I'm sure every woman here would like to bang him. They've

banged everyone else."

"I'm not really interested in that right now," I said. "Lately, I've had more ass than a toilet seat. But if Snoop sees something he'd like, well, I'll just drink and mind my own business."

"Red," he said, "I have to tell you something. Once you done it with Wild Winnie, there's no one else who even comes close. I'm being honest with you. She'll make you so horny that your cock will explode."

Snoop then spent the next couple of hours reviling his wife, Jaylene, and how she threw things at him and cussed him out over the most trivial matters.

"Red," he told me, "can you imagine how I felt when we were out at some restaurant and Jaylene went ballistic because I wasn't paying enough attention to her? She threw a glass of water in my face and ran out of the restaurant because she thought I was ignoring her! She's done everything from taking the scissors to my clothes to smashing my big-screen TV with a heavy pot."

"I have to ask the obvious question: Why don't you divorce her?"

"I can't. The legal fees are too high. But I stay away from her because I would rather freeze to death in the back of my car than be

BRIAN ANTONSON

henpecked to death."

I told Snoop that I would love to drink with him some more but I needed to make some important phone calls, one of which was to Sheri.

Snoop shrugged and said, "Send me the whole manuscript as soon as you think it's remotely publishable. I think time is the main thing now, seeing as how people are talking about you so much and want to know more about you."

I said goodnight and went to get my car in the parking lot. There I saw a girl get out of a Mustang. She was chomping on gum and trying to smooth out her too-short dress. She reminded me of Jaylene before Jaylene let herself go.

"Are you the one they call Wild Winnie?" I asked her.

She stopped and squinted at me. "What's it to ya?"

245

I left Bayporte and flew everywhere to go on TV and radio talk shows and the luncheon circuit to tell everyone to live a clean life and buy my book. Unfortunately, not everyone listened to me.

In one city, I met a pretty woman who told me she was there because of a convention and we ended up in bed together. Afterwards, she demanded three hundred dollars from me. I didn't know prostitutes had conventions. And she wasn't worth three hundred dollars, either.

In one Southern city they kept asking me if my teammates used performance-enhancing drugs.

Some conventioneers insisted that I go bowling or play badminton with them. Other times, I got calls at my hotel by people who wanted me to go out to the suburbs "for a ball-busting good time."

Somewhere in Dixie, I checked my emails and found a message from Flash.

R&S,

I'm still out here, learning as much as I can about everything. Have you ever studied up on the American Civil War? It's a fascinating thing, and you can look into it all you want via the miracle of the Internet. I know we're all Canadians, but as wars go, that one was totally vicious and completely captivating.

People who smoke dope all day don't get much done.

You two should get married and have many beautiful babies. Maybe name your first son for me. Does "Flash Crossley" sound good to you? I may drop by for Christmas dinner one of these years, so keep a place set for me.

Go Invaders!

A fan forever

I read Flash's email over the phone to Sheri and said, "I really hope he doesn't get caught with drugs."

"Yeah," Sheri said. "You know what they say about overseas prisons?"

"Tell me," I said.

"In the shower, don't bend over to pick up your soap."

As I concluded my speaking tour a few days ago, I called Sheri to tell her I could catch a flight back to Bayporte late that evening.

"It's been wonderful," I told her, "but now I have to get back home, where people don't talk funny."

I asked her to meet me at Eli's, and I would entertain her with tales of my life on the road and at the podium.

Instead, she met me at Bayporte International Airport with a Canadian Comfort over ice in her hands. I took it from her and drained it in one swallow, then hugged and kissed her.

"I have an idea," Sheri said as we walked to the baggage-claim area. "I've been thinking of all aspects of human life, as bad as most of it is, and I have concluded that the only hope for us is to become lovers."

We kept on walking and I didn't say anything.

"Hello?" she said. "Is anybody home?"

"I'm home. I'm listening," I

said. "What do you think?"

"About…?"

"About our becoming lovers." Then, "You may think I want you to become my lover as a way of retaliating against Flash Gortton. Remember him?"

"Kind of."

"But you know that I'm not a retaliatory kind of person, so my interest in you is genuine. You also know that I'm terribly horny these days and you and I could work out some sort of sexual relationship so that if Flash ever did return, which he probably won't, he wouldn't even know about, assuming that I would still want him when he *did* return."

I stopped for a moment to grope for my baggage-claim tickets. "Keep talking," I said.

"Well, it's just that I've been so wounded by Flash's disappearance and you two are the only people I've ever really felt close to. I'm not sure I'm thinking straight and I've been so lonely, but I think that you and I would make a good couple."

"A good couple, eh?" I said, staring down into my plastic cup of Canadian Comfort over ice, which was just ice now. I kept hoping it would magically refill itself.

"Red, I'm trying to be serious. You're the only person I've ever had any use for, and vice versa. For all those years, it was Flash for fucking and Red for many other things. I think we should give fucking a try."

"I wonder if, by some miracle, by luggage actually made it here to Bayporte," I said.

"You and I love each other, Red. Don't deny it. I love you and you love me. I kept wondering why I could never like any of those Francesca Roff-type bimbos you were always humping, and now I understand. It was partly that they simply weren't good enough for our little circle, but also that they were with you, and I wanted to be with you, too. They were standing in my spot. I've always had a claim on you as my own personal possession, so it pissed me off when you were banging someone else. Of course, I was banging Flash all the while, and that must have made me look like a hypocrite.

"Lately, you see I've been really horny for you. I've been thinking that, in addition to your other terrific qualities, maybe Red Crossley is a great lay!"

On the drive back to our apartment, and while we sat in Eli's and ate, I tried to tell Sheri why her idea of us together would make both of us nothing but miserable. There was always a chance that Flash would return, and even if he stayed away, Sheri and I could only destroy our friendship by getting into a big sexual thing.

"All you need to do," she argued, "is pretend I'm a new chick. Someone you haven't balled yet."

"But you aren't. You are my friend Sheri Rawson from Bayporte. We've known each other forever."

She started playing kneesies with me under the table of Eli's and said, her voice smoky and slutty, "Jack, you can call me Jill. Where you come from, anyway? Aw, don't matter. You guys are all the same."

I don't know why, but I consented to play Sheri's weird little game. Soon we became sweeties, even though I wasn't sure what Sheri Rawson expected from *me* as a boyfriend. Flash had an easier time as her guy; he just acted like himself.

I laughed at it all at first. We went to every Bayporte restaurant, nightclub and movie theatre. We saw one movie after another that I slept through, and the "golden topping" they put on the overpriced popcorn tasted rancid.

Sheri and I decided to stay home one evening so that she could fix me one of my favorite meals, a cheeseburger the way they make them at Eli's, with Canadian cheddar and back bacon.

I would be lying if I said that her burger was as good as Eli's, but she did her best for me and that's what counts.

We had drinks before, during and after, and drank coffee spiked with Grand Marnier. Then we lay together on the sofa with the TV on and stared at the screen without paying attention.

By and by we turned our attention from the TV to each other. We stared at each other for the longest time.

She said, "Don't say anything."

I did as told. I just stared at her some more. She looked at me as if I were someone new, not good ol' familiar Red but some new man she had met out here in Hawaii and she was trying to figure me out.

I ran my hand through her blondish hair, then caressed her neck. I wanted to make some smartassed remark about us, but she wanted me to shut up, so I did. What I also did was to kiss her long and hard, the inappropriate but gratifying kiss I had given many Francesca Roffs.

I kissed Sheri the same way, again and again.

Soon she rearranged herself so that she lay across me on the sofa. She stared at me, then frowned and smiled. She caressed my face and shoulders.

We kissed each other more and more, and we clung to each other as if we were a couple of teenagers going at it in the backseat of a car at a drive-in movie theater while hearing the voices of managers or cops or whoever banging on windows and ordering kids to stop their funny business.

I stopped our kisses just long enough to say, "I think you're right. We may be able to make this work out."

"Shut up and kiss me some more," Sheri said.

www.ingramcontent.com/pod-product-compliance
Lightning Source LLC
Chambersburg PA
CBHW080804120626
46556CB00009B/3219